Carnival of Reality

Allison Whittenberg

Apprentice
House Press
Loyola University Maryland

First Edition

Casebound ISBN: 978-1-62720-380-7
Paperback ISBN: 978-1-62720-381-4
Ebook ISBN: 978-1-62720-382-1

Printed in the United States of America

Design by Katie McDonnell
Edited by Amber Davis
Promotion plan by Amber Davis

Published by Apprentice House Press

Apprentice House Press
Loyola University Maryland
4501 N. Charles Street
Baltimore, MD 21210
410.617.5265
www.ApprenticeHouse.com
info@ApprenticeHouse.com

Contents

Ride the Peter Pan

There were times when it seemed like all the beauty was sucked out of my life. This was one of them. It was cold and damp, early spring, and I was Greyhounding from my old life to my new, from North to South. I was 24, master degreed, unwed, and pregnant.

All around me, I saw failure. As each passenger climbed aboard, emptiness filled the bus. I saw the unshaved and the unshowered. The angry and confused. Widows, retirees, practically invalids dragging their duffle bags. Beside me, a degenerate unwrapped his plastic wrapped sandwiches. I stared out of the windows like a peeping Tom. Riding the bus never meant passing City Hall, never going by the nice restaurants or boutiques melting into friendly pedestrians strolling past. No businessman with wedding bands checking briefcases. No, I saw a squeegee man dirtying clean windshields.

I wish I'd taken the Peter Pan, a special line that showed escapist movies. I'd taken that before when I was only going as far as NYC. I saw a flick about moving an elephant cross-country. It wasn't a box office smash but for a bus ride it was perfect. Here, there wasn't even a blank screen. I could go for another feature length; too bad that line doesn't go down South.

A man with eyes like the sky was doing the driving. He loud talked to the passengers in the front couple of rows about how fake pro wrestling was. He asked the question, "How come every time they hit each other, they stomp their feet?"

Back in high school, I was valedictorian. A decade later, long after Pomp and Circumstance was played, I found myself a loser. Just another confused minority waif riding public transportation bouncing the back of her neck against a greasy headrest…

My wish was for a miscarriage. I know that was a horrible thing to wish for.

I had used up all my distractions. I put on my headphones and heard only a staticky cassette tape. The magazines I had brought, I had read too quickly. I had put away the novel I had brought miles ago. I just couldn't get into it. It was just words on a page. Now what?

There was a woman with chicken wings in her shirt pocket. Her fingers smudged the window.

I'm going to kill my baby. Strangle it with my large intestine or with my hands like the Prom Mom. It was a fleeting thought. I blamed it on the bus. Some people get motion sickness; I get homicidal thoughts.

If only the Peter Pan would go way down to Georgia. Maybe I should have flown or rented a car. Truth is, I didn't have the presence of mind to do either. I needed to let someone else do the driving. Let someone else make the stops and turns. I was so angry. Angry at rape, domestic violence, the porn industry, sexism, fascism, racism, ismisms. My life wasn't supposed to go like this. I was the smart girl.

I should have watched my drink.

I should have reported it.

I should have taken the morning after pill.

I shouldn't have been in denial.

RU486 could have stopped this from being compounded. How am I going to look at this product for the next 18 years? How? What am I going to do? Where am I going? I know where I'm going. Macon. But *where* am I going?

I'm going home. I don't even have a job waiting for me. I had two grand saved; that's all.

My legs were cramping from a rocky night when I tried to turn this seat into a sofa. I snuggle in the best I can.

I had no other plans than to live with my mother. My mother was loving and nurturing but not understanding. She couldn't understand this; I couldn't understand this.

A few rows behind me that Lolita pop music was playing, someone else turned on a hip hop station and overpowered it. This all could have been understandable if I dressed like that naval centric nymphet, but I didn't. I never did. Even on that night, I had on my work clothes at the party, Navy skirt, light blue turtleneck. (When groping for cause and effect, fall on stereotypes.)

I thought I knew Warren. We had talked before about peace, public education, and reparations. My life was going so well. I was saving to buy a condo, something tasteful with modern furniture. It would look like the furniture storeroom at Ikea. Now look at me, boomeranging back to my same humble beginnings, to the grey borough I grew up in. I have lost control. My power is taken. My destiny. Couldn't he at least have opened up a condom package and put it on?

The woman in front of me was babbling about how thick her son's neck is. He was in the Navy and that Navy wanted to kick him out because he'd gotten fat. They have been taping his waist and throat to find the density.

My rapist wasn't big, but he did overpower me.

My rapist didn't look like a rapist. He was tall, slender, a runner's build, dark, bookish eyeglasses—kind of like me only male and a pervert.

I only had one glass of wine.

Date rapists aren't any different from rapist rapists. In a lot of ways, they are worse. They gain your confidence, then betray you. They Milli Vanilli their way into your life. They don't carry a knife or a gun. Just a drug. And surprise.

I remember my stockings pulled down around my ankles so I couldn't move my feet and run. The wheel of my mind takes in the way he braced my arms, so that I couldn't move my arms and clock him. The way he got inside my mind so even my voice didn't work. Why didn't I scream? I lived in an efficiency on the third floor where the walls and ceilings were as thin as loose-leaf paper.

I worked in the politics of shame as a counselor at a women's shelter where the politics of silence was busted every day. I should have come forward. Instead, I did what I urged others not to do, I swallowed it down… yet the projector kept whirring and clacking.

There was a woman on the bus with her hair so uncombed she had dreads from the neglect. Her carry on was a shopping bag full of pain. I was just like her. Up until the rape, my life had been so fine toothed combed. Pregnancy dictated to me that all my dreams were gone. Even my distant ones of going to Africa, eating raw cashews in Nairobi, tracing my roots . . .

The bus driver stopped just past Columbia. He told us to get a smoke or a coke. The previous day, I had thrown up twice. Today, I was hungry. I went to the restroom to wash up. The smell of joints hit me as did the sight of women brushing their teeth and washing up. Not just bird baths. Not just splashing under the armpits, spritz to open the dry eyes. These women had their tops off and their pants down. They were buck-naked crowded by the drain.

I left the rest room and cleansed my hands with a moistened towelette I had stored in my carryall bag. I ducked into the terminal coffee shop and sat at the counter.

A waitress made her way over to me and grunted at me.

"Do you have any turkey?" I asked.

"No."

"What do you have?" I asked.

"Burgers. What did you want? A club?"

"No. I wanted a Rachel."

She looked at me blankly.

I explained. "It's like a Ruben, but you use turkey."

"We don't have no turkey."

"Do you have bacon?"

"Do you want a BLT?" she asked.

"No. Bacon cheeseburger."

"We don't have no cheese."

I squinted. "No cheese? No bacon?"

"Nope. So what do you want?"

"An abortion."

She gave me a blank stare.

"I'll have a burger," I swallowed hard and said hoarsely.

"You want fries with that?"

Soon, the moon-faced waitress slid the plate my way.

The bun was cold, and the burger looked like an SOS scouring pad.

I just don't get it; I had done everything I was supposed to do right down to only using my first initial on the mail and the phone book. How did I get raped?

Some fellow with a head full of shiny Liberace hair—every strand in place -- sat next to me. I eyed him. He was a brown skinned man, chubby, I don't know why I thought Liberace. I should have thought Al Sharpton.

"How's your burger?" he asked.

I said nothing.

"My name's Brian." He smiled. I noticed that he was missing a side tooth. "You know, you are exactly what I'm looking for."

I thought for a moment; exactly what was I looking for? A life of fox furs, red sequin evening dresses? White candles in silver candlestick holders? The man kept smiling at me showcasing his missing molar. I told myself to give up. Life is not going to be gallant.

He chewed his burger favoring one side. "What's your name?"

"Ann." I lied. It was really Arna. This is what I always did. I never give strangers too much information. Even in singles clubs, when asked for my phone number, I would give only the last digit. I'm always cautious, watchful.

"Ann. I like that. I like women like you. I like a woman whose breasts are where they're supposed to be and have a nice small waist like you have."

I turned away from him and placed my napkin over my burger.

"I have a truck," he said.

I put a five-dollar bill on the counter.

"You want to go for a ride in my truck?" he asked. He smelled oily and close.

I stood up. "How old are you?"

"I'm 42, but I don't want no has beens. My daddy had kids up until he was 60.... I don't date women over 21, 22."

"You don't."

"Naw, I don't want a has been."

"Do you have any kids?" I asked.

"I have grandkids," he answered.

"You have grandkids." I absorbed and repeated.

"Yeah, but that's my daughter's business."

"What happened to your wife?" I asked.

"What wife? I've never been married – " He leered. "- Yet."

I made a fist. "You're a 42-year-old grandfather. Why don't you date grandmothers?"

"I done told you I don't deal with no has beens," he told me. "Have you started your family yet?"

"By family, you mean a mother and a father and a child right. If you mean that, the answer is no." I made my voice icy as Massachusetts in December. I kept my cadence proper and dry.

"You know what I mean. You got any shorties?" he asked still snagging a toothed grin.

"The answer is no."

I turned to leave. He reached for me.

"Get your goddamn hands off of me."

The entire clientele craned their necks at me. An older woman next to the door looked over her glasses at me. The waitress cupped her hands over her face.

"I went to Smith!" I told them, then I gave Grandpa the finger.

I gathered my coat around me, clutched my bag and walked toward the pay phone. I had promised I'd call my mother when I got close to home. I pulled out my card and pressed the digits. Ma answered on the first ring.

"How's your trip going?" she asked.

"All right," I answered. This was my biggest lie yet.

"It's a cast of characters ain't it?" she laughed. I loved her laugh. It was full, colorful, and Southern.

"How far are you along?" she asked.

"Right outside of Columbia."

"How far are you along?" she asked again.

"I'm right in Sumter. Outside Columbia, I'll be there in another two hours."

"No, Arna, how far are you along?"

"You know? How could you know?"

"I just do. Something about the way you told me out of the clear blue you were moving back home. You love Boston."

She didn't sound angry or disappointed. She sounded psychic.

"Everything is going to be all right. You're not around any smoke are you? They say that now. That ain't good for the baby."

"I'm only two months in, Ma," I told her.

"It's too bad you have to travel pregnant. You have morning sickness and jet lag."

I smiled. It felt strange to smile. "Ma, you can't get that from a bus because you feel every mile."

"Buses ain't so bad anymore. Don't they show movies?"

"Certain ones do. Greyhound has a spin off. Peter Pan. I'm just on the regular one."

"Well, you'll be home soon. We'll all be there to pick you up."

"I don't have a job lined up."

"You're a mother now. That's your job."

"But I had a career."

"You find something down here. You've always been smart."

"Ma, I let a dumb thing happen."

"You're the first one in the family to ever go to college, Arna. You'll find something down here. We got everything's Boston's got. Just a little less of it."

I saw a mass of people heading toward the bus. "Ma, I have to go."

"See you soon."

The bus was just about to pull off as I climbed back aboard. The driver asked me if I knew The Rock.

I crossed my fingers and said, "We're like this."

There was a reshuffling of the seats, and I found my middle of the bus seat gone. I went to the back.

It's always those honor student, 16-year-olds who don't want to disappoint their parents who hemorrhage from grimy abortions. Ma took the news better than I thought.

My mother had emphatic ears. She didn't wear makeup or nail polish. She had basic hobbies; she liked to sew and cook. She was lucky; she didn't go out to the world to discover herself. She was married at 15. I was the exact middle child of seven. Maybe. Macon wouldn't be so bad, it's not like I had a job on Wall Street. There're shelters in my hometown or at least people in need of shelter.

A voluptuous big-hipped woman sat next to me. She had swollen ankles. She was one of the nude women I saw in the restroom.

I guess I wasn't put into this world to be pampered; I was put in this world to be squeezed between a window and foul-smelling misery.

Back home, kids ride their bikes and chase each other up and down the sidewalk. Just thinking of that made me feel warm enough to ignore the draft that was coming from the metal vent alongside the window.

I will not end this life.

If it's a girl, I will cover her pigtails with red and purple plastic. If it's a boy, I will teach him to be kind.

The bus started up, and I got a mild case of whiplash caused from my neck bouncing against the headrest.

There are times when it seems like all the beauty is sucked out. This isn't one of them.

Think Warm Thoughts

The world burns. The sun stalks.

Can life be sustained off a window sill's moisture; a lead pipe's sweat? Someone spills the orange juice we've been rationing. It spread more sunshine across the room. We splintered our tongues lapping it off the wooden floor.

In the white glow of night, a man bursts in and steals thirty-three ounces of water.

I should have shot him, we're all going to die anyway this way.

As want drips into need, it's a good news bad news sort of thing, contentment, comfort.

It's all a matter of degrees, I am between cool white sheets. Outside snow is falling, falling, falling like sugar. It's piling up to hills, mountains.

They say a new Ice Age is upon us, but my fever is breaking and I remember a wise, old saying.

The Sane Asylum

Coop hammered at her front door. Lucy heard the knock and entered the living room. She wore a fitted red dress under a loose white apron. She opened the door.

"I think you know why I'm here," Coop said. "I'm here on behalf of the United States government with a notice for your son. Is he home?"

She slammed the door.

He knocked again.

"Mrs. Jackson, Mrs. Jackson," he called. "You're just prolonging the inevitable."

She went to the central closet and took out the vacuum. She began using it on the thinned oriental rug, bumping into the hodgepodge of rummage-store brown furniture.

"Mrs. Jackson. Mrs. Jackson," he called over the noise.

She turned on the radio. He banged harder on the door.

She ignored it.

He went to the window. He lifted it and climbed through.

"You really ought to lock that. Anyone can climb through," he told her.

"Any criminal."

"Mrs. Jackson, I'm not a criminal. I represent the United States government."

She spat at him.

He wiped it off with a handkerchief from his pocket. His voice remained low and impersonal. Wide shouldered, he was a good-sized man with a proud carriage. He kept his small brown eyes behind army-issue glasses.

"Kentu Jackson is your son, right? He needs to report to— "

"I've never heard of him."

"Kentu Jackson is your son," he stated.

"I said I've never heard of him."

"Ma'am, this is no time to play games. Every able bodied man between the ages of —- "

"He's not going."

He handed her the paperwork. "Here. Here's the address of the armory. If you need transportation, call this number and transportation will be provided for him."

"I said, he's not going," she said and ripped the paper in half.

He opened up his bag and pulled out a roll of tape. He taped the paperwork back together. He told her, "Well then he'll be put in jail. Have your son show up on the 22nd. That's the way things are." Coop stiffened. "I'm sorry."

"Are you?" she demanded.

He noticed that her eyes were done up. Kohl blackened that he had only seen in movies by white actresses. This effect played just as dramatically against her brown skin. "I said I was," he said.

"You know, my father died. He was a marine."

"I'm sure he died a hero."

"He's dead all the same," she told him. "How many homes do you visit a day?"

"You're my eleventh," he told her.

"It ain't even noon."

"I'm highly motivated."

She winked at him. "That I can see. Tell me, what kind of reception are you getting?"

"A little of everything. Some people are like you."

Her eyebrows raised.

"No matter. I'm trained to deal with all kinds."

"The old country doesn't work anymore. I hope you know that the public doesn't want this."

"That may be true, but everyone has to do his parts. This sacrifice must be shared equally. It isn't like there's some mythical French Foreign Legion that's going to handle all of our business. It's up to us. All of us. Do you have any cash?"

Her dark eyes roved over to him.

"Get some cash together. Have about a month's worth on hand. Get your documents together. Get a sleeping bag. Make sure you have enough kerosene for a lamp."

"Did you round up the two boys on Cherry Street?"

He looked at the list.

"What's the last name?"

She thought for a moment. "Williams. I think."

He nodded in affirmation. "Yep. Vincent and Joseph Williams, 2441 Cherry Street."

"How about that other boy?" She snapped her fingers as she tried to think of his name.

"Can you be more specific?"

"He's about my son's age. He has a funny-shaped head." She demonstrated the way he walked with his shoulders up close to his ears.

"You'll have to give me a name or an address."

"Cherry Street, too. A little bit up the block."

Coop checked his sheet, his nostrils fluttering slightly with his indrawn breaths. "I have a Lawrence Tucker. He's on 2713 Cherry."

"That might be him. How about —"

"Don't you communicate with your neighbors?"

"I don't get out much."

Coop looked around at the bare, textured walls but kept getting back to her. Clothes were on the radiators. Dust balls were the size of borders. This cretin was housed in the corners. Books were strewn everywhere. That body, so strong, so healthy looking, soft, large breasts above a tapered waist above wide, feminine hips.

"My advice to you is to start communicating even if you don't like it. We have to stay connected and create a network."

"What are you talking about?" she asked.

"Survival."

She gazed at him with a lively expression. "Would you like a cup of coffee?"

He scratched his head. "Coffee?"

"Yes. Do you like coffee?"

"You're offering me coffee? Mrs. Jackson, I'm talking to you about emergency preparations."

"How do you like it? Black or with cream and sugar?"

"I like cream. I have to go."

"What's your rush?"

"I have a schedule, Mrs. Jackson. Make sure your son gets that letter. It'll keep him out of a lot of trouble."

She smiled. "One coffee with cream coming up."

Coop's military bearing was all but blown. "Mrs. Jackson."

"I'll put it in a Styrofoam cup. You can have it to go."

Coop made a notation in his logbook. Lucy tried to snatch the book from him. He pushed her away.

"Can't you wait five fucking seconds. It's just a goddamn cup of coffee... I'm sorry. I'm sorry. I don't get much company."

Coop imagined her kitchen. More chaos. Coffee boiling, sputtering to the top of the pot, staining the already stained walls. Much like this living room, the kitchen was probably a very dark room. Grime choked out the light. "Mrs. Jackson, I don't want you to go to the trouble of making a whole pot."

"All this is missing is a woman's touch."

"What are you?"

"*I'm* a fucking lady." She smiled and leaned into him. "What do I look like?"

He shook his head and smiled sadly. "You really ought to get some fresh air, Mrs. Jackson."

She gazed at him heartily. "A recruiter. A survivalist and a shirk all in one. This is my lucky day... How old are you?"

"Late 20s. Knocking at the door of 30."

She told him she was pounding on the door of 40. "I wouldn't be against war if they took people my age and up. The roster when my father had died, the median age was 22."

"The young fight better. A geriatric soldier ain't much use to anybody."

She nodded. "They take the youngest and the strongest."

He frowned. "Long as they don't take the brightest—"

"My father was 19 years old."

"He must have started early."

"Which one, having a kid or dying?"

"It's a good thing he did reproduce early. If he didn't, I wouldn't be here. If I weren't here, I wouldn't have given birth to my son. And you would have him on your list. Isn't life funny that way? The 22nd, is it? You're going to take my son away."

He tilted his chin up. His jaw stiffened. "I'm not taking your son away."

"The hell you aren't, soldier. I blame the messenger for the message. There is no need for this war. We can talk this out."

"We have tired of that."

"We could try some more. Offer another resolution."

"You know what you remind me of, Mrs. Jackson, that scientist from *The Thing*."

Her face crinkling into a game lopsided smile. She told him there was no scientist in *The Thing*.

"Yes, there was."

"No, there wasn't. I saw that movie the week it came out. That was when I used to go out."

"How could you? It was made in the '50s."

"It was made in the '80s," she insisted.

"No, it was a black and white film."

"Soldier, it was in color."

"We're talking about two separate movies. In the film that I saw the soldiers have the thing surrounded, and they are about the fire at it. Then this scientist comes running up to the soldiers to stop them. The scientist said, 'Wait a minute. Wait a minute. Maybe we could talk to it.' So the scientist goes running up to The Thing and The Thing knocked him in the head."

"That doesn't happen in the remake. There's no scientist."

"Don't tell me, The Thing doesn't get killed?"

"Yeah, they killed it, but it still ends kind of dark. They're stuck on this remote Arctic wilderness in front of a dying fire.

After they kill the thing, they all think they are safe but then they remember they have no way of getting back to civilization."

He asked her what the thing looked like.

This time her cheeks raised with her smile. It radiated lines to the corner of her eyes. "Great special effects. Each time the Thing gets shot it morphed into a dozen other things. Sort of like our foreign policy. The future can be changed. It doesn't have to be war."

"Mrs. Jackson, war brings peace."

"War brings peace?" she repeated making his statement a question. "People call me crazy. After killing The Thing, we're all going to find ourselves huddled around a dying flame. My son is not going to fight in your war. He's a conscientious objector."

"He didn't register as one."

"I didn't know he needed to. He's at a peace rally right now. He's a pacifist."

He gave her a pseudo smile. "So am I."

She smiled. "You don't dress like one."

He smiled more fully. "What do you have against the military?"

"It's not so much the military. It's the government."

"This is the United States, Mrs. Jackson, we are the flame of democracy. I'll do this much for you. I'll report that you were nowhere to be found. That'll put him on the bottom of the list. It'll be a month maybe even two before the next go round. By the time there's a next go around, maybe it'll be over one way or another."

"Thank you. Thank you. I knew you weren't a monster."

She reached to embrace him.

He stepped back.

"I'm just trying to thank you."

"You don't have to. Just tell your son to be careful at these peace rallies. A lot of people get hurt at them."

"You make it sound like war."

"It's worse than war. They are prolonging things. Your son honestly thinks if he speaks to enough people he could stop the war?"

"My son is a peace fighter. Couldn't you take him off the list all together?"

"That's all I'm going to do for you. I've got fifteen more houses to get to. I want to get to them before the curfew."

"I'm going to jump out of the window."

He pointed to the window he came in through.

"Make sure, it's that one. There's not much of a drop."

"I'm talking about killing myself if you take my son away from me."

"Ma'am, I did what I could."

"But I'm suicidal, I tell you. Don't you have a pamphlet in your satchel? Some referral list."

"There's nothing else in my briefcase for you."

"You've got very nice brown eyes. They're very kind. Understanding."

"Mrs. Jackson. I really have to leave now."

"Don't they usually send you fellas around in groups of two?" She asked running her fingers through her loose afroish hair. Her black hair shone like a newborn animal.

"The short story is we're very short handed."

"Do you think they'll send my son to the front?"

"What front? There is no front. In case you haven't noticed, we're surrounded from all sides."

"You're gonna put my son in the middle of all that."

"Mrs. Jackson, we're all in the middle."

"He's my son. My only son."

"This is just the way things are. He's got to go. Sooner or later we all will. The William brothers. Tucker with the funny head and walked like this down the block. Lottie, Dottie, every damn body."

Lucy's kohl eyes looked sad. "My son is anemic."

"We'll feed him steak. Medium rare."

"He's vegan. He doesn't have the temperament. He's my only son. Isn't there a clause against that?"

He stiffened his lips. "Not any more." He turned and walked to the door.

"Wait. I want to tell you something. I'm not a Mrs."

"I was just being polite."

"Polite? What, are you from the Midwest?"

"Texas."

She brightened. "Oh, a Cowboy. Well, I'm surprised you don't sound as cornpone like our leader. Can you say nuclear?"

"I never had much of an accent."

"Just say it."

"What?"

"Nuclear."

"Ma'am please. I don't have time --"

"It's kind of funny. He said nu-clear. Nu-clear. Well, I think it's funny. Here we are on the brink of nu-clear war." She laughed and those crow's feet sprang up on her face.

"If he'd like us to believe it, it would be nice if he could pronounce it."

"How many times are we going to go through this? Being lied to, manipulated by our government with these scare tactics."

Coop turned to her. "What makes you so sure this is a scare tactic?"

"What makes you so sure it isn't?"

"I'm an MP, ma'am. I follow orders."

"You're being lied to by this war machine --"

"I have a job, Mrs. Jackson."

"No war for oil."

"That's not what this is about."

"What is this about? Does anyone know?"

He said nothing.

"I thought you had an answer for everything."

"I don't have an answer for that."

"You are a nice-looking young man. Are you spoken for?"

"Mrs. Jackson."

"I done told you, Cowboy—I'm not married—yet."

"Ma'am."

"Call me, Lucy."

"It's short for Lucia."

"Lucia," he repeated.

"I like when people call me, Lucy," she told him, she went to the door.

"I'm going to stand in front of this so you can't leave. I'm going to be a human shield."

"There's always the window. That's how I came in," he told her.

"I'll be a human shield there too."

"Ms. Jackson…"

She grinned.

"I'm a priestess. I'm going to put a spell on you."

As Coop tried to make sense of her words, Lucy was all over Coop. It was too late for reason. She was kissing him.

Pawing him. Her dress screamed the color red. She took off her apron and Coop's glasses. Then began to take off her dress.

The next morning, Kentu was on the telephone. He was a short man with a hollowed chest and knobby knees in baggy canvas trousers. He paced as he spoke. He had his mother's big, dark eyes, sans smudged mascara. On the front of his tee-shirt was the word *Peace*. On the back it read *Bush Is A Mother Fucking Cock Sucker*.

He talked into the phone. "Yes, the buses will leave at seven in the morning. Yes, it's $20 per seat but no one will be turned away due to lack of funds. We need as many people there as possible to declare to the world that this war is not in our name."

His mother, Lucy entered. She is in just a beige slip which played warm against her deep skin tone. "Kentu," she said.

"Hush, Ma…" He went back to the phone. The voice on the line told him that 5 am was too early. "Our government is about to unleash the full military might against another third world country don't tell me 5am is too early in the morning. What? Huh? Take a goddamn nap on the bus then."

"Kentu," she called.

He waved her off. "Not now, Ma."

In his intensity his shoulders bent forward. "We can't think of our own physical needs right now. Think of the Iraqis. They have suffered over a decade of war and sanctions. Think of their sacrifices. Think of the Afghans, they don't even have alarm clocks. They don't have beds. They live in abject poverty and squalor. What?" he asked the phone. "What? I don't care if Seattle is closer, we want to be on the big one this weekend. What? Yes, the San Francisco one is bigger. Yes. All right, all right, we'll leave at 8 then. Is that all right? You spoiled American pig get your fucking beauty sleep... And don't forget BYOS...Bring Your Own Signs."

He slammed down the phone.

"What do you want, Ma?"

"I just wanted to say, good morning."

"There's nothing good about this morning, it's the same old America with the three KKK. The same old economical plunder enforced by military genocide from the Congo to Kashmir. From fucking Chechnya to the fucking Sudan –" He up and downed her. "Where's the rest of your clothes? Don't tell me you got some last night."

She giggled. "All right, I won't tell you."

"Who is it?"

"You'll see."

"He's still here. Well then it can't be the newspaper man. He'd have to be on his rounded by now. Is it that carpet guy?"

"You'll see."

"It's the carpet man."

Coop walked in the room; he bristled at the sight of Kentu's tee shirt.

Kentu's jaw also dropped. He even staggered back a bit. Both men peered at each other in a moment of silence. Kentu spoke first. "A white pig with black skin. Ma, you have really scraped the bottom of the barrel this time. You bring this slime into this house."

"Slime?" he asked the words turned in his head. Synapse fired. He looked at Lucy.

"Well, you two go on and get acquainted."

Kentu pointed. "You're lower than slime. You're a puppet. Just like that manufactured enemy by the mobilization of xenophobic political reactionary flag waving patriotism. The pressed uniforms. The shiny shoes. The fruit salad on the chest. Trinket medals. This is an outrage. You are such a fucking joke," he told Coop. He then called to the kitchen. "Goddamn it, Ma. You are damn desperate." Again, he pointed at Coop. "You're not the first and you will not be the last. Over the course of 19 years I've seen the newspaperman, the carpet guy, and three mailmen. All those poor brothers fell for that crazy lonely bit. Ma, you better bring back that plumber to lay his pipes, because this is totally unacceptable."

"Coop, how do you like your eggs?" Lucy asked from the kitchen.

Kentu paced, eyes flashing. "This must be some kind of fucking joke."

"Scrambled, it is," Lucy said.

He pointed to the kitchen. "She can sleep with whoever she wants. I've got bigger things to worry about."

"You're impeding ship date?" Coop asked.

"I'm not going anywhere. If all goes right, neither will you."

Coop ignored the bitterness in Kentu's voice and tried to carry on a normal conversation. "Diplomatic roads have been exhausted."

"Have they?" Kentu asked. "There's still time to talk. I'm joining the blockade. Thousands of us are going to form a human shield."

"You can join hands with your mother."

Kentu shot him a quizzical look.

"You're wasting your time."

"No one said peace is easy."

"Some people make things harder than it has to be. I'll just say goodbye to your mother and leave."

"You don't have to. She is famous for these etch-a-sketch relationships."

Coop went toward the kitchen.

"Don't flatter yourself, Soldier. I told you my mother had plenty of visitors. You can leave without saying goodbye."

Coop halted and looked at Kentu. "I was flattering your mother."

"You know what they say about bread. A slice of a cut loaf is never missed."

Lucy came back in with a tray of steaming eggs, home fries, and toasted toast. "Breakfast is served. Coop, why don't you sit here next to me," she instructed.

"He'd rather have a mess kit and crawl under into a foxhole."

She clapped her hands. "Kentu, you sit here."

Kentu stared at the plate contemptuously.

"Who can think of food at a time like this? I've got to get things together for the noon rally."

"Be careful. I know what kind of madhouse peace rallies are."

Kentu scowled. "Like you would ever know."

"I've been stuck trying to police them. Y'all act like you've lost your minds."

Kentu banged his fist on the table. "We're peaceful god-damn it!"

Lucy said, "Boys. Boys."

"You're the warmongers, "Kentu told him.

"Kentu, be nice to our guest," Lucy said.

Coop said, "You're wasting your time at those rallies. Laying down in the middle of the street like some damn fool. Time is at a premium. You should spend all of your time preparing. "

"You're the one who needed to prepare," Kentu said.

"I am prepared," Coop said.

"Oh, yeah. How much water do you have?" Kentu asked. "How much duct tape do you have? Are your windows sealed up? Tell me at all those checkpoints do you even know what you're checking for? Do you really know what the enemy really looked like?"

Coop up and downed him. "Yes."

Kentu ruefully pointed at him with his grimy, bitten up fingers. "Get your own affairs in order. You got a lot of nerve coming over to people's houses trying to tell us. Who do you think you are? "

"My MOS is --"

"Don't give me that Army talk shit."

"That's the same way my father spoke," Ma said.

"You never met him, Ma, he died before you were born. The US army killed him."

"What do you mean the army killed him? "Coop asked.

"Exactly what I said. We've given enough to this country," Kentu said.

"I'm getting sick of your 'I gave at the office' way of thinking. I'm sorry about your father, Lucy. This is a whole different thing now. This country needs--"

"Fuck what this country needs. This country brought things on itself," Kentu said. "The United States has a habit of selling weapons to both sides. My grandfather. In his last letter, he told of how he was Made in the USA was on every bomb. They sold the bolts and nails that went into the weapons that killed us. We've cornered the market of weapons of mass destruction, Soldier. But you don't believe that. Dare I call it a conspiracy?"

"Conspiracy?" Coop said. "You don't get it. We are in it. We are in it. After everything is settled and calm, we can sit around and sort through each and every point you want to bring up."

"You don't understand --" Kentu began.

"No, you don't understand. Here's a headline that you'll never read, 250 million Americans did not take part in a peace march today. There's a fire that we have to put out. You want to go over the history of fire and all the right and the wrong ways that fire has been put out through ages. You're not going to be happy till we are all charbroiled with all your discussions and your marches."

"Like Grenada, out of 5000 trooped they awarded 800 medals. That's better odds than any lottery. More medals. More fruit salad," Kentu said.

Coop waved him away. "Go beat a bongo drum."

"You are just like the red coats. You are the enemy. You support this bullying rapacious "friend". We will derail this globalization movement. Waving an American flag won't make it go away."

"Your methods are just as calculated," Coop told him.

"Warmonger," Kentu snarled.

"War will bring peace."

"That's the craziest fucking goddamn thing I ever heard, " Kentu said.

"You talk that way in front of your mother."

"I'm calling you a motherfucking asshole just like anyone who puts on a uniform is an asshole." Kentu stepped toward him. "Now what are you going to do about it?"

"Nothing," Coop told him, still in a flat tone.

"The pressed uniform. The shiny boots. The fruit salad on the chest. Trinket medals. You are such a fucking joke. "

"You're the one in the uniform," Coop said. "That tee shirt is a disgrace."

"Coming from you, that's a compliment."

"You're the tool. You may as well enlist in Saddam's Army."

Kentu nodded. "I'd like to. At least he has some standards. Some ethics. I stand with Saddam Hussein and every other oppressed person."

"Oppressed?"

"Look at the history of this country. Terrorism. Rape and pillage. That is the history. You have the never to join this army to rape and pillage."

"Hey," Lucy spoke up.

"Stay out of this, Ma."

"I'm the aggressor," Lucy told him.

"You don't want it. Not from him. You only think that you do."

Lucy said, "I do."

"Why don't you go to a singles bar?" Kentu asked Coop.

"I came here to do a job," Coop told him. "I have a summons for you."

"Take that conscription notice, wrap it around your anthrax vaccine, shove it up your ass."

Coop frowned. This angry, frothing, freezing dog of a man with furrowed brows and filthy clothes. Coop tried to maintain his military bearing. "I'm going to forgive your words on the count on your youth."

"Forgive me? You ought to hang your head in shame for representing this country. You don't understand!" Kentu screamed. "I WANT TO LIVE IN A COUNTRY THAT'S DEMOCRATIC AND HUMANE. NOT THIS PUPPET REGIME. THE PEOPLE OF THE MIDDLE EAST ARE NOT THE ENEMY. POVERTY IS SOARING THERE AND HERE ALL THE WHILE WE ARE --"

"What do you care about programs or people?" Coop asked.

"Programs help people. Every dollar of the 200 billion they are spending on this war. Libraries are cutting their hours."

"What will the homeless people do during the day?" Lucy asked.

"They have less acquisitions," Kentu said.

"You're talking to me about library books?" Coop asked.

"Our war planes attack helicopters and kill innocent people every day."

"Save it for a pamphlet."

"I'm saving it for you."

"I don't want to hear it."

"You are in my house," Kentu told him.

Coop told him. "I'm in your mother's house."

"So what does that mean? I can't talk, huh? You're silencing me. You're taking away my first amendment rights. You're not here to talk; you're here to fuck my mother."

Lucy said, lifting her bowl. "More scrambled eggs."

"Every other nation is against this," Kentu said.

"If that's true, that's not my concern. Even Kennedy said, "Let every nation know it wishes us well or ill, that we shall pay any price, bear any burden, meet any hardship, support any friend, oppose any foe to assure the survival and success of liberty."

"Black soldiers, white wars. The chocolate front. Decades of foreign wars. Your raw naiveté manifested in utter blindness. You're primitive scraping your knuckles across the ground."

"Wrong again. We have the most well-mannered, well-equipped standing army in the world," Coop said.

"Once again, once again a predominantly white society chooses to send its black male population to fight a war that was distasteful to whites. And we don't disappoint, we give them frontline participation. And you, you deliver us to them. As if we haven't given enough to this country."

"That's the first point you've made so far that I agree with, Kentu."

"I've got more information than that. Draftees aren't even cost effective. They account for 30% of the deaths in Vietnam. I'm taking in the county."

"In country?" Coop asked. "You ought to worry about the city. You say you are so concerned about Black people. How many drive bys are there? How about the infant mortality rate? How about the school shootings? That's the real war zone."

"How do you know? I thought you were from Texas," Lucy said.

"They got cities there too. Houston is the third largest city in America."

"I bet there are a lot of flags waving there. Bunch of gun toting flag wavered pickup trucks driving Billy Bobs."

"Do I look like a Billy Bob to you?" Coop asked.

"No," Lucy said.

"Ma, control your glandular yearnings." Kentu said. "I'm talking about the disproportion utilization of African Americans."

"There is no conscious or unconscious effort within the government to conspire to fulfill the ranks of service with African Americans," Coop said. "I think that the underprivileged and unemployed and the poorly educated should stay that way. Stay right where they are, don't learn new skills. If your father was causality of war that should make you want to make things even. It is your duty to protect the nation."

"Do you feel protected in this country, Black man?"

"If what you're saying is true, it's true in military or civilian clothes."

"If?" Kentu asked. "You know it's true."

"Now is not the time —"

"When is the time?"

"After this is over. That's obvious," Coop said.

"Obvious to who? After this is over, we will be in the same dungeon we've always been here in Amerikkka with the three kkks."

"I don't see what racism has to do with this."

Kentu said, "You don't want to see what racism has to do with this. You're blind. You and your army uniform and conscription notices and your lies."

"You're the one who's lying."

"That's your advice to me?"

"You've got your draft greeting. Do what you think you have to do."

"I will not," Kentu said. "I will not capitulate."

"Like I said do what you have to do. All men of a given age group have entered the draft roles. This isn't the Revolutionary

War. It's the 21st century. Whites don't pay 300 dollars to be released from service. We are all called up."

"I'm not going."

Coop told him, "Then run. Go to Mexico or Canada."

"That doesn't work so well anymore."

"It worked well enough."

Kentu told him. "Draft dodgers need funding."

"If it's all that important to you—You'll find a way. Look at Bill Clinton, he was from a poor family, broken home. He's a good role model for you. He promised to join the ROTC. Instead, he ended up in England as a Rhodes Scholar running down this country."

"No government really rooted in limited parliamentary democracy should have the power to make its citizens fight and kill and die in a war," Kentu said.

"If you're quoting Bill Clinton, finish the quote it all the way. 'A war that does not involve immediately the peace and freedom of this nation. The draft was justified in World War II because the life of the people collectively was at stake.' At stake. We are all at stake.'"

"Like Hell we are."

"I guess those two buildings tumbled down on their own."

"White people are at stake. Not us."

"What?" Coop asked.

Lucy spoke up. "He said, 'white people are at stake. Not us.'"

"He heard me. That was an attack against the government not us. But thanks to sellouts like you, the misery will be spread to us. Thanks to you, caskets will return filled with the remains of African Americans."

"No blacks died in the World Trade Center? Or the Pentagon? Huh? Where's your answer to that?"

"I just gave it to you."

"You are so confused," Coop told him.

"I assure you my thinking is clear."

"Maybe you're thinking clear, but your talk is full of shit."

"You're the one that's brainwashed, Soldier."

"I am an African."

"You are an American to them," Coop said.

"Them is us," Kentu told him.

"Us is us," Coop shouted. "And they are them."

"They really got to you. As the sun glistened off your armor, Gunga Din. Go ahead fight for the empire. Meanwhile, us indigenous minorities can't even get a meal at Denny's. The British/ the Germans/ the French in Africa. The Fucking Portuguese."

"What century are you talking about?" Coop asked.

"While they lulled us to sleep with all their men bitten by shark stories and senator sleeps with intern crap, all this was being plotted. Our government --"

"Stop right there."

"Just like Pearl Harbor. It's true," Kentu said.

"NYC. DC. This was the worst day in the history of our county."

"I guess Rosewood doesn't count. How about Black Wall Street? How about the bombs in Birmingham?"

"We face biological, chemical—We didn't face that in Alabama. For Christ's sake, what do you want to do to leave Jihad factories to incubate to another 10 years?" Coop asked.

"You don't really believe that bullshit about 10,000 luscious virgins for them in heaven. I'll tell you why they kill; they have nothing to live for. They call them sand niggers."

"Who's they?" Coop asked.

"This country is chronically racist, sexist, homophobic."

"I'm not. I'm just trying to do my job. And stay alive."

"Your job kills people. You make sure people are signed up to go halfway around the world and make things go boom. Your hands are drenched in the blood. The blood of other people of color. Other brown people getting robbed of their land. America must be stopped. Stopped. Before this world is like us. Starbucksed. Big Mac Fucked. The world is not for sale. This pernicious, oppressive, depraved. Gunboat diplomacy. The world is wasting away by our foreign policy. We don't give a shit about nonwhite non-American lives. One barbaric military intervention after another Somalia, Haiti, Bosnia. Supporting tyrants. Despotic marauding multinationals. America is messier than a barrel full of monkeys. You want to avoid terrorism? Do you?"

"Stay away from tall buildings and white people. If you do those two things, you will be alright."

Coop said, "That's it. That is it." He rooted in his briefcase for Kentu's taped together paperwork then ripped again. "You don't want to go, Kentu. Don't go."

"Don't think there's not a backup somewhere in HQ."

"I don't want that boy over there with me. He might shoot the wrong direction."

"Who are you calling boy?" Kentu asked.

"Are you leaving?" Lucy asked.

"Who are you calling boy?" Kentu asked again.

"You're going over there?" Lucy asked.

"Who are you calling boy?" Kentu asked.

"Kentu, leave Coop and I alone for a few minutes." Lucy told her son. Coop noted as he exited the room that Kentu with his scrawny body didn't even look like he was part of the same species as his lusty built mother.

There was a long heavy silence between Coop and Lucy. She said, "You didn't tell me you were endangered of being shipped, Coop."

"What do you mean I didn't tell you? I just met you. There's a lot of things I didn't tell you."

Lucy screamed. "You just met me. You just fucked me. When is your ship date?"

"Lucy, this is not --"

"Don't tell me. Don't you tell me what this is or this is not. When do you ship? "

"Calm down first," he told her.

"Answer my damn question."

"Not until you calm down."

"What difference does it make if I'm calm or not?"

He went to the door.

"Where are you going? Where do you think you are going?"

"This was just a temporary assignment. I ship on the 26th.

"That's too soon."

"My mission is to secure --"

"I don't want to hear about your fucking mission."

"No, I guess you don't."

He turned to leave.

"Wait. Wait. Will you wait one minute? Give me. Give me. Give me. One minute of your time."

She carried his glasses.

"On the nightstand, you left this behind. You must not need them."

"Just to see things at a distance."

"I have great vision. I could have gone to flight school. Clear. 20/15."

"You mean 20/20."

"20/15," Lucy corrected.

"20/20 is perfect."

"20/15 is better than perfect."

Coop reached for his glasses. She held it just out of reach.

Lucy tried on his glasses. "You know what they call these. BC glasses."

"Before Christ?"

She laughed. "Birth control because they're so ugly. You've been in it for a while; you must have heard that."

"I guess."

"BCG's, I hope they worked last night…"

"You told me you were menopausal."

"I lied."

"Just give me the glasses," he told her.

She took them off but again held them just out of reach.

"I used to be just like you. Nearsighted. Then I took a course."

"A course?" he asked.

"An eyesight course. It was only two sessions. Thirty-eight dollars at the Upper Moreland Learning Tree."

"What do you learn in an eyesight course?"

"I just told you. How to see. If you're bad at it. You have to train yourself."

"You trained your eyes to see for 38 dollars."

"Plus a five dollar material fee."

"What kind of material?" he asked.

"An eye chart. I remember the day I had my breakthrough I had been practicing my eye lessons all summer long and it all clicked for me."

She covered one eye and mouthed the letters. "X J L A 2 R Z."

She covered the other eye. "X J L A 2 R Z. It was a miracle...Not really. It's not really a miracle. All I do is trace around the edges of things. I don't really see things. You see, seeing is psychological."

"Lucy, seeing is seeing."

"No, you just think it's here." She pointed to his eyes.

"But it's really here." She pointed to his head. "You see, Coop, maybe there's some things you don't want to see. Maybe there's some things you like to remain fuzzy."

Coop nodded. "All I have to do is believe, and I can change the shape of my eyeballs."

"All you have to do is believe, and you can have anything you want. Believe, not wish. Believe. I believed that I would meet someone special. Someone I could connect with and talk to. He came right to my door. I didn't wish I believed, Coop. Believe me those other guys are just guys. You are what I believe in...." She licked her lips. She came toward him. "Do you have to go? Do you really have to go? "

"Lucy, I have orders."

"I know. I know. You have orders from headquarters. When they say jump, you say how high.... Well, here, take your glasses."

He took them but didn't put them on.

"Can I give you something else?" she asked. She took off the beige silk scarf from around her neck and handed it to him.

He smiled thinly. "It's very nice."

"I hope it reminds you of me."

"Thank you."

"Just one other thing. Take this."

She took off her gold ring from her right hand. "It's my grandmother's wedding ring."

"You're giving me your grandmother's wedding ring?" he asked.

"For luck."

"For luck."

"You're repeating what I said."

"I can't take this," Coop told her.

"Take it."

"I can't. You keep it."

"Take it. Take it. Take it. Take it to some foreign land. Afghanistan. Uzbekistan. Isbucastan, but I don't understand why I must take a stand in some foreign land-- Get the clap from some whore. Go ahead, take it. Please," she shouted.

He headed for the door.

"Coop. Wait. You haven't had breakfast. Can I wrap you a muffin?"

Coop walked faster.

"Coop, wait. Wait. Wait. Don't open that door."

Lucy ran to the drawer and pulled out a gun. Coop turned to her, quizzically then his eyes connected with the weapon.

She cocked it, then laughed hysterically. "You're not going, Coop."

"Where did you get a thing like that?" he asked.

"I've always had it."

"I didn't ask you that."

She continued to smile venomously as she triggered the gun. "In this world of uncertainty, a woman needs some protection."

"You don't see me aiming anything at you, Lucy."

"Well, that's the problem, Coop."

"Put the gun down, Lucy."

"I've got you cornered. Hemmed in like a UN Peacekeeping envoy."

"Drop it!" he told her.

She laughed again. "You know the funny part about this. I don't know where my father drew his last breath in. The village. It's not even on the map. I couldn't find it. Forty years later, Nam is a tourist trap. You can book a cruise to it. That's what will happen to Baghdad. The same thing will happen to Isbucastan. What the hell is an Al Qaeda? Huh? What's a Jihad? I don't know any of this? I don't Osama Bin Laden from Oksana Biau."

"Where did you get that gun?" Coop asked.

"It's Kentu's."

"Kentu? The peacenik?" He stepped toward her.

"It's Kentu's, and it's loaded. I'll prove it. I'll shoot up in the ceiling."

"Then you'd have a hole in your ceiling. Just put down the gun."

"Don't reach for this," she warned him. A little froth was at the corners of her mouth.

Coop squared his shoulders, silently and charged her. He grabbed her gun arm and when he got that, Coop took the gun from her. They struggled only briefly. Lucy was scratching, slapping, cuffing, ripping, and tugging at Coop.

He aimed it for the ceiling and fired, surprising himself by the kick back. "It is loaded."

"Now, I have a hole in the ceiling."

Kentu comes downstairs and charges at him. Coop fought him off with one belt, an uppercut that sent Kentu soaring for the roof.

Coop's voice rose and got wild as theirs. "Stay away from me, both of you, you're crazy."

Kentu came back to his feet. "Look who's talking. You shot a hole in the roof."

Lucy looked at the ceiling. "Look at it as extra ventilation."

"Like it's hot in here," Kentu said.

"I was sweating bullets," Lucy said.

"What in the Hell are you doing with a weapon?" Coop asked.

"You said it yourself. Those peace rallies are no joke, " Kentu said.

Coop said, "I'm getting the Hell out of here."

"Coop, no, I don't know what I'm doing I'm so crazy with—"

"Let him go, Ma."

Lucy pleaded, "I thought I was in the country. I'm suffering from shell shock. You can't leave me, Coop. You belong to me. You belong here. You can't go there and live in a tent. You need a home. You don't have a home. You've got a base. You've got a unit. You've got three huts and a cot. I'd rather shoot you then let you go out there and die. Die anonymously. For some, vague notions of freedom, justice — equality."

"The kind of freedom, justice, and equality we have never known," Kentu said.

Coop aimed the gun at them. And all but fired it. He was that demented by the moment. Bestial. Vicious. He had almost forgotten he was in full uniform. *Sanity is a relative term. It means different things to different people at different times.*

"Stop, both of you."

Both mother and son backed up.

Coop opened the weapon and took the bullets out. He placed the empty gun on the table. He grabbed his bag and exited himself from the house. He left, slamming the door behind him.

Glory

In war time, you marry a man who is tall and stalwart.

You marry a man with a sullen smirk. You don't marry a soldier; you marry a partisan. One of the rebels, a hard-core. And for a few days every now and then, life is interesting.

Aussie is your husband and he is also a thief, taking advantage of the kind of bottomless chaos that only war could breed. He is young. He is alive. He is full of pride.

He often disappears for weeks at a time. He sends no word. He spares no words. You have two children. You mother them when you can. You work as a maid to get by. Though you've never been to school, you can read, but not very well.

He brings you glory when he comes. Spoils from the War. Glowing jewels. Religious medals. He tells you how many thayers he can get after he larks them. You get excited. A smile spreads across your face like butter. Your eyes reel in marvel as if you've never seen such a collection of shiny babbles in your whole, entire life. You finger through the pile after he dumps it on the grubbery table. Aussie pulls up a chair and together you ogle at every last gem.

"Shit!" you exclaim. "What did you do Aussie, light-hand every last homeowner in the New World?"

He gloats big instead of answering you. You want to see him without his clothes on.

He is a beautiful man. Built tight and showy like one of those Old World Greek statues. And he has thick lips that kiss you sometimes as soft as summer. He has thick lips that kiss sometimes hard and still it is magic.

He grabs you in all different places.

He puts you into all different positions.

He doesn't bother to take off all his clothing; he is only interested in seeing you stripped.

Now your body is beneath him. Black waves brake with a white slap then a roar. You hold on. He is wild and strong.

The next morning, you wake up next to him. You are a wet leaf soaked by the rain: moldy, plastered to the doss cover. You look over at him, he is waking up too.

You kiss him for a while and for a while he kisses you back, then he pushes you away. He heads to the washer. He returns in a few moments half changed into his quasi uniform: a tee shirt, blackstrides and hiking boots, not all the way dry from last night.

He says to you, "The take I brought last night ain't nothing like what I'm fixing on pinching. I'm swinging over by that border city tonight."

Thinking it is just as well, you shrug. You've got to pick up the kids from you mothers. You've got to be over at the Ulms by nine to clean their bath, straighten out their closets, make space.

Outside the white snow is falling, falling, falling like sugar. You watch it through the window, piddling away the few moments you have left with Aussie.

Just as Aussie leaves, you ask him when he will return.

He surprises you and says he'll be back in two days.

You do not cry, but you want to. You don't tell him how lonely you are. How scared you are. How much you think the war will never end. How much you think you are losing your looks, wasting away, going insane.

All you tell him is that you love him.

And he gloats big.

You ask him to kiss you. One more for the road. He does. He kisses you sweetly; he puts his heart in it.

Why Didn't You Call Me September 11th?

Jean's body was drawn up in the cold. Her eyes traveled the room. Frugal, Tim kept the thermostat at 54. His nose was often red, right at the tip. It made him look like a drunk. She looked down the corners as she wondered for a moment where she was. She had one of those soprano headaches — huge and pulsing.

Her brown body was on one side of the bed. His white one on the other. Not touching. Not on her belly. Not on her thigh.

They were quarreling and while they did Jean looked at the four walls. They were blank. The one picture he did display was downstairs. It was a bike trip he took when he was in college. She never asked him why that was special enough to put up but she guessed it commemorated back when he thought of the city as an adventure instead of a cesspool.

"Jean, my brother said you should have called me."

"You weren't even in New York," she said.

"I was in an airplane."

"You were in North Carolina."

"I was *over* North Carolina."

Tim Flanagan was taller than her. Nearly 40, he wasn't handsome anymore. Fallen-faced. He played golf for recreation, and his body wasn't thin or thick. It was simply prematurely middle aged.

Jean was average height. She kept her hair well straightened with Dixie Peach and always looked somewhat older than she was. It was the gray hair that she did a lousy job at concealing. She had a block in the front that was solid white. Very much like Tim, with his salt and brown hair and his stiff gestures, his droopy, damp eyes, she wasn't trying to appear youthful or vigorous.

They had other things in common. Neither liked to do much. It was always dinner or a movie. Never both. Tim always paid but never bought her flowers, stuffed animals, or candy. He thought that was wasteful and meaningless.

Tim worked as an engineer, and Jean was a psych aide in a ward for abused children.

They both went to bed early in order to get their eight hours of sleep each night.

Intercourse once every other week was all right. Clothed intercourse with the lights off lasting only minutes in the standard position. Both were partial to quick kisses. Neither liked the tongue.

Jean shivered. "Well, why didn't you call me? Why didn't you check on me? All those kids I work with. I had to keep them sane."

"You know I don't have your work number."

"You never asked for it, Tim."

"I never needed it. You have your mom if something really happened."

"And your brother lives right down the street."

"And he called me."

"To ask if I called you?"

"No, Jean, he called to see if I was all right like you were supposed to do."

Tim came from a good-sized Irish Catholic family. His mother, also just two miles away in the house he grew up in. Two married sisters in Delaware.

"If I was living with you, I would have called you," she said.

"Why would you move in here with me? This is an hour from your work."

"We could live together in some place."

"I'm not selling my house. Not in this market. And what about your mother? You can't leave her alone after all these years... So where are we going, huh?" He sounded irritated. The icy range in his voice. "Jean, what if I said I will marry you tomorrow?"

A white chill bit through her. She folded her lips.

"You wouldn't ask me that."

"What if I did? What if I said, 'Jean, let's get married'. What would you do then?"

He turned to her. "Look, maybe I'll get that new position. I'll be able to telecommute. I'll also make about $10,000 more."

"Then we'd see more of each other?"

He lapsed into thoughtful silence.

They lay silent as if watching a dying fire. No chasing after each other crying. The arguments they had were never operatic. They were always like this, carefully modulated.

She pulled the covers more tightly over her nightgowned body. He seemed fine in his flannel pjs. Some people are like that, climatized.

The next morning, Jean drove home, looking without watching, without seeing.

She thought of all those glossy vacation brochures she'd been collecting, fantasizing about their imaginary honeymoon where they would both finally splurge and live it up. She'd also been scoping at children with olive complexion and straight hair. That's how her pretend child looked. Straight-haired. No turn at all. She wasn't a racist; she just liked that look. She believed it was prettier.

Jean never thought she was particularly pretty. Her thick eyebrows dipped into a V. All throughout high school, her mother wouldn't have let her pluck her eyebrows. If her mother would've let her pluck her eyebrows, would she have been more popular back then? Those were the crucial years for forming relations. All of the expectant widows of 9/11 seemed so well connected. Well into family formation when it happened. Several were into their ninth month of pregnancy.

She stopped for gasoline and a Snowball. Jean liked to write down everything she spent through the day right down to the sixty-six cent cupcake purchase. In her whole life, she'd never bought a bottle of wine or dry-cleaned an outfit. She had cassettes. No CDs. That would mean buying a CD player. Her clothes were from Clover's. Sensible shoes, not too much heel. She really hadn't changed her simple style of dress from 20 years ago.

The sugar and carbohydrates plateau took away her headache. Up until that day, Jean had thought that he was the one. They had so much in common. Both were conservative people. Though it was mid November and they'd been going out over a year, Tim wasn't her boyfriend. They didn't share. She never left anything over his house or felt like she could – should

When Jean reached Calhoun, the small, nondescript borough on the outskirts of Philadelphia, her mother was about to leave for Presbyterian Church. Her blue haired, gossipy friends were about to come by for her. The house was roasting. Her mother liked to keep things at 77, fussing at her anytime she touched the thermostat. Jean immediately took off layers of clothing till she was just in an undershirt.

Jean stirred some Tang into a glass of water and put the Eggos in the toaster.

"Why don't you have some oatmeal today, Jean?"

"I don't want oatmeal."

"You have waffles every morning. Have pancakes. It's almost the same."

"I want waffles, Mom."

Jean's mom had shiny black walnut skin and a Jeri curl wig that she started to wear after a bad relaxer.

"What movie did you see? Did you see *Collateral Damage*? Is it worth it or is it a rental?" she asked her daughter.

"It was all right, Ma," Jean answered.

"I thought they were holding that back because of all this."

"They did. It was originally supposed to be released back in September."

"Well, I guess enough time has passed. Here it is November already. Does he get the terrorist that killed his family?"

"Of course, Ma. That's Hollywood."

"I wish you would have waited to see it with me, Jean. I like Schwartzenagger."

"We can see the next thing he's in, Mom."

Jean was an only child; the product of her father's second marriage. She had half brothers and sisters that were in their fifties and a whole cadre of half nieces and nephews who lived from 200 to 1000 miles away. It was hard to keep in touch. Her happiest days were behind her when she was really young watching her father adjusting the Windsor knot of his tie. Wrapped in a quilt of her father's memories, missing his large, big knuckled hands – his laughter. He liked coconut covered marshmallow filled cupcakes. It was adult-onset diabetes he died of. He kept his sickness from her. He was that kind of father.

Jean reassured herself that Tim wouldn't break up with her with the holidays coming. He was sensible enough to save the trouble of looking for someone new. So, another whole generic year went by almost and Jean and Tim were on the same tepid schedule. Once a week dinner or movie/ sex barely touching. But it didn't feel like the relationship was winding down. It was just settling down like a stone at the bottom of a river. Eggos and Tang. Day after day, Jean went to work, came home and spoke to her mother and went to bed.

International news varied in the next few months. It was either about anti-terrorist military squads or the INS or whatever. Yet it never seemed like the culprits would be precisely identified.

Months later, the bad guys weren't captured. They hid in caves. Jean didn't read the *New York Times*. She watched TV and Peter Jennings told her and her mom about Afghanistan and other countries she'd never heard of. What was Al Qaeda? What's a Jihad? This vocabulary. This geography.

Ten months passed, everyone was still asking deep questions about kismet. What's kismet?

Jean wanted to find a new job, but was unable to locate the resolve to do so. She didn't even want to be in the educational field anymore. She never did. Obedient and logical, she had done beautifully in high school, but less so in college where her brand of spewing back exactly what was dictated to her wasn't so well rewarded. Her paper would always come back with the same advice 'Put more you into this."

She should have gone to forestry school. That's what she really wanted to do, but there were so few women in the field and even fewer blacks. As a consolation, she volunteered at an animal shelter Saturday mornings and afternoons. She liked feeding cats and dogs. She liked helping the approved applicants in selecting just the right dog for adoption. She had her eye on a Labrador retriever mix. Just two months. Dogs stay in your life for a decade or so. It'd be like a marriage. She ran the idea past her mom.

"I don't want some dog," her mom said.

"It's a small dog, Mom."

"Who's going to clean up after it? You? Look how you keep your room."

Jean listened to her mom as she'd always done. Her mom was now in her 70s. A little stooped, she took tablets for her osteoporosis. It was her house. Jean just lived there with her. Her mother set the thermostat high, saying old people have old bones.

The first September 11th was on a Tuesday. This time it fell on a Wednesday. Jean called Tim.

"Hi," she said.

"Hello," he said.

"I just wanted to call you."

"What? Why?"

"Because I didn't last year."

"Oh, that. You're still thinking about that. That's ancient history. I'm glad you called... I have to go away this weekend. So we can't get together."

She thought of how it would be like laying in bed with him. Not touching, not looking at each other in their frozen divorced compartments.

"Isn't it funny? Your brother got married to that girl who he'd known for six months less than you'd known me."

"That's funny?"

Jean was burning up in this hot house. "I didn't get to the punchline–they still haven't found Bin Laden."

"You're acting strange."

"Aren't you going to ask how work was today?"

"You never asked me. Look, where is all this going, Jean? You call me in the middle of this week, and you're all over the place."

"Have a good trip, Tim. I'll see you the weekend you get back."

"Now you sound like yourself, Jean. Good night."

Then he hung up. Then she hung up.

It was only eight in the evening. She looked around the room to see horse posters on the wall. They'd been there since 6th grade. Jean walked downstairs.

Her mom was on the couch. Sunday paper is still out. Metro section strewn. A 9/11 retrospective of local residents lost. Coupons clipped.

Her mother had coffee on a saucer. No longer hot, luke-warm. Cold. Jean wondered how she could stand sipping at it. Cold liquid that was supposed to be hot.

Her mom had her hands on the remote scanning the channels. Press the bottom on the control, and the image faded.

On this anniversary, Jean didn't want to be alone. She went to the kitchen to have Ritz crackers with peanut butter then she went to the living room to be with her mother. A sofa and two armchairs formed a U around the TV.

"I guess nothing regular's going to come on tonight," her mother muttered.

A young, hot Latin singer did his hit single. Something about being a hero. It was clear that his vocal ability was lacking. He made it on his appearance. Tall, olive, romantic looking.

"What kind of variety show is this?" her mother asked.

Jean sighed, leaned in the doorway, and turned her eyes toward the set. In that chunk of time after her father passed away and she had started going out with Tim, she questioned life. Obviously, those who die young never grow old, but how about those who grow old who never had the chance to be young? Jean was young when her father passed.

Jean wanted a new life. She wanted death to be the one that she had. With any death, there would be rejection of the truth, depression from the truth, acceptance, then the reconstruction part. She needed to change towns and jobs. She needed to buy a place to live on her own. But she didn't want to live alone. She couldn't.

When her father died, the world didn't stop. TV shows weren't preempted. Balding, overweight, always had a smile, joked a lot. He used to bring home Chinese food and Chinese tea and say "Take tea, and see." Upon his death, her legs buckled under, face frozen in disbelief. His laugh, big, throaty and full. He was the life of the house. He lived 72 years six months and twenty-two days.

Jean's heavily lidded eyes watched the TV. She thought that she could try to find someone else on the internet. Log on under her America Online handle. Her middle name followed by the number 2. Perhaps she could meet someone who actually wanted to share. To get married and have a child and a dog. To start something that would be there. Always.

It was the pop opera singer's turn. The way this woman sang was so emotive and clear. She reached her arms and delivered a song from the musical *Carousel*. "You'll...never... walk... alone..."

The camera panned the audience of blacks, whites, youngs, olds, gentiles, Jews.

The audience nodded in affirmation. They turned to their sons and daughters and sisters and brothers like this was just what they needed to hear.

Jean's right ear touched the flat cushion. Her shoulders sagged. She felt life pass her, and then she felt nothing.

Just over the Moon

On that blue-sky day, there she was, Nikki Joval. Nervous and shaking, I saw her. She wore a lace inset tank top, low rise corded denim jeans, and a crochet wrap as a belt. With her long legs and lifted posture, she didn't look like she was supposed to look 33. She looked 23.

Men eyed her up and down.

As I approached her, she smiled warmly. She kissed me full on the lips, hugged me, and told me that it was so great to see me.

I was more reserved. I put much less into the hug and didn't kiss her back.

She guessed over me, saying how long she'd been anticipating my visit. My body's resources were still reeling from the plane ride, and I couldn't give her anything.

As we made our way outdoors, I didn't expect summer air or all the accented people of color. There was a Pakistani looking skycap and a Mexican looking shoe-shine man. Africans worked at the food court. "Where did these people come from?" I asked her.

"What?" Nikki didn't follow my line of questioning.

I let it drop. Back in April, we had exchanged dates. We spent so much time together growing up. We'd stand on the corner of Horizon Drive and talk for hours not wanting to leave until we'd said everything.

I hadn't had a friend like that since she'd left Pennsylvania. Since then, everyone seemed so busy with jobs or school or rushing home to catch TV shows.

"You know where we are, Jean? We're right by the Mall of America." She then said, "It's the --"

"I know it's the largest mall in the world," I cut her off.

Nikki said she was going to tell me about the roller coaster and that she'd always taken her daughter Melody there.

My luggage of two Samsonites fit snugly into her Dodge, which was cluttered with stuffed bunnies, jazz shoes, tap shoes, trainers, and rosary beads (her mother was Catholic).

She hadn't changed. Nikki still auditioned for company after company. Still tried to make up for the time that she had to take off to have Melody, which had set her career back. Ironically, that year, she was offered a spot in a company. She made her living in a piece meal. She taught at five different places: the Hennepin Arts Center, Minneapolis Sports Authority, Russo Dance Center, and the Modern Jazz Conspiracy. Her passion was tap, but most companies didn't have much enthusiasm for it.

I thought I should ask about how her daughter did when I did. Nikki smiled broadly and began gesturing. "You know what she's into?" she asked me.

I turned to her. "Drugs?"

"No, soccer. She'd rather hit the ball off the top of her head than dance. Can you believe that?"

"I thought you were going to say drugs."

"No, I'm not really worried about my Melody getting into that. My daughter and I talk. We always talk." Nikki laughed and went into the slogan: "If you don't talk to your children about drugs someone else will."

I looked out the window: this was the land of 1000 lakes. It looked pretty much like the part of Pennsylvania we were from. Overhead in the intersection, the traffic light turned from green to yellow to red.

"You're following too close behind that car," I told her.

"Sorry," she said.

I hadn't seen her dance since we were in high school. I remember her dance style was like a tropical breeze.

Her place was up the fire escape, three flights and over three doors. Her home had the faint odor of vanilla. She had flowers in various states of health.

Her place was cluttered around the edges, open in the center. Red corduroy curtains should have been unchanged from the winter. I looked at the schedule that she had hanging on the fridge. "You teach dance classes from nine in the morning to nine at night?" I asked her.

"Only on Fridays."

"No wonder you stay so skinny," I said.

"Jean, can I put in the tape?"

"What tape?"

She said that she danced to the music of Pearl Harbor and recorded it. "I liked what it had to say about friendship."

"*Pearl Harbor?*"

"Yeah. Those two characters. I forget their names. But that opening scene when they're just kids, and they sneak off in the plane together. Then when they join the Air Force together --"

"Nikki, *Pearl Harbor* wasn't about that. *Pearl Harbor* was about Pearl Harbor. The sneak attack that led us into WWII."

"And it had a love story."

"Yeah, but that wasn't true."

"I'm sure something like that will happen. Hawaii is a big place."

She put in the video. In her wicker chair wrapped in a cocoon, I watched. "You followed your dream. I gave mine up years ago."

"What were yours?"

"You know."

"No, I don't. I don't remember you ever --"

"It's stupid. I wanted to be a forest ranger. How many black forest rangers do you see?" I asked her.

"Don't think like that. Where would we be if we thought like that? Jackie Robinson would have stayed with the Monarchs. You can be a forest ranger. You could be out there with Yogi Bear and Boo Boo."

"I guess if it's not dance you can't take it seriously," I told her.

"Then why don't you do it?"

"I can't now. I'm too old."

"Do those schools have an age limit? Lie about your age then."

"The program I wanted is all the way in Denver," I told her.

"So move."

I frowned; she didn't understand anything. "I'm too old for that."

She opened a bottle and poured two glasses. She raised her glass. "To us."

"I don't drink wine."

"Just a sip," she urged me.

"I tasted it."

"It's shiraz," she said.

I pushed the glass toward her. "I don't want any."

"Come on just a taste."

She put the glass to my lips. "No, Nikki."

She pushed a cork back into a bottle. "So tell me what else is going on in your life?"

"Not much. I'm thinking of getting that guidance counseling certification. Oh, and I met this guy through Match."

"You met a guy!"

"Yeah, but –"

"That's wonderful! What is he like? What's Match?"

"Never mind."

"No, tell me."

"Never mind, Nikki." I changed the subject. "What class are you teaching tomorrow?"

"Pilates."

"I didn't know you knew Karate," I said.

"No, Pilates. It dates back to Joseph Pilates. All the Hollywood stars do it."

"Do you have a *TV Guide*? What time does *Survivor* come on, here?" I asked.

"What's *Survivor*?"

"Two teams of people. In a jungle. They perform tasks."

Her eyes fluttered then her eyebrows arched. "Like what? Do they ride elephants?"

"No, it's more like what they have to eat. Maggots and –"

"Maggots! Fried? And this is on TV? My Melody's a tomboy, but I think even she'd draw the line at maggot eating. This show must be on cable. I can't believe that show has people eating maggots on TV. What's that thing Clinton was going to put in the TVs to protect children?"

"I don't know." I turned on the TV just in time to see the show's final credits roll. "I missed the show."

"Awww," Nikki said, making a sad face. She went into the next room and came back holding comp tickets.

"I thought we'd hit a club."

"It's 9pm."

"The club's don't get going till eleven."

"I'm really tired from the flight." I folded out the plumb chocolate colored sofa. I changed into my night clothes.

Nikki came back into the room. "Oh, I see, you're ready to go to bed. I was going to let you have my bed."

"This is fine."

"Or Melody's."

"This is fine."

"Are you sure?" She sat on the edge of the fold out.

"Nikki—"

"You know what I was thinking. I was thinking about England. In England, they show full frontal nudity on TV. But in this country, take a look at the talk shows every time you turn around you see some saying 'Seek Hail'."

"What?"

"You know what I mean. I mean what is more offensive the Klu Klux Klan or a woman's nipples."

I winced.

All things change, and all things stay the same. The next morning, I went into the bathroom. The shower curtain was open. It was there that I saw Nikki with a man. His shoulders were touching hers. His warm hand full on her taut and bare breasts. His other hand's fingers firm on her behind.

For a moment, I thought I was dreaming, but my dreams were never like this. My dreams were flat and unmedicated.

"Jean," Nikki said. I closed the door.

The next time I saw them, he had on a towel. He was a skinny guy, made of edges, bones jutting out in all angles. He must have some dance in his background, or, at least, running. Nikki was in panties and a tee shirt.

He got fully dressed then left kissing her on the lips before he left.

"Who's he?"

"Miguel. He's from my night class. I asked him if he'd come out with us tonight."

"I don't want to go out tonight."

"I thought you didn't want to go out last night?"

"Nikki, I want to get settled."

"I got you the Eggos. Remember when I asked what you like to eat for breakfast and you said Eggos."

"I guess you're going to make fun of that like my mother always does."

"Nope." She smiled and began to fix my meal. For herself, she prepared yogurt and strawberries.

"That must be how you stay so skinny," I told her and asked her where she'd kept the syrup.

During her class, her body was like a feather floating. All about me, other women were hollow as flutes. Their taut overworked body thrusted in pelvic tilts and shoulder bridges. Diamond dogs. Pilies. I watched Nikki walk on her hands forward keeping her legs and arms straight until she was in a pyramid shape. Her head hung free, ponytail flipped upside down.

I walked out.

"So what did you think of the class?" Nikki asked, when she saw me waiting by the lockers.

"I left."

"I know you did. What you saw of it, was it good? Did you like it?"

"It was fine, Nikki."

"I like this gym better than my last one. You couldn't go a second over-schedule. This fitness center is a little more laid back. I can --"

"It was fine, Nikki."

That night, I went to bed early again.

The next morning was Nikki's bank loan meeting. She apologized about a hundred times that she couldn't reschedule.

"Nikki, do what you have to do," I told her.

She wore a cropped top and yoga pants.

"Where do you shop for clothes like that?"

"No place special. Sometimes I go to Nicollette Mall. Sometimes I go to Rosemont Mall or The Mall of America. Melody likes the roller coasters there." She babbled and was happy bright as the sunlight glinted.

The bank's waiting area featured plants of all sizes. I pulled a *Newsweek* from the display rack. My mother subscribes to it. Condoleezza Rice was on the cover. It was familiar and calming.

"Come in with me," Nikki asked.

"I'll wait here," I said.

"It'll be fun."

"Nikki, this is a bank."

"Miss Joval," the attendant called.

"Are you sure you don't want to come?" she asked.

"Positive."

She added a little skip to her step. That gets up. That goes.

She stayed seated, talking to him for a good while. I peeked over to watch and caught her hands wild gestures and the fortyish, salt and pepper buzz cut personal banker's face amused, intently listening to her.

I missed my TV shows. I missed the regularness of my life. She wasn't who I remembered and then she was. She was still the one who cheated for me on a 10th grade Spanish test. It was the last question on the pre-test; the incentive is that if you get everything right you didn't have to take the real one.

Grades were very important to me. Not so much to Nikki because she always expected to have this great show business career.

"Guayabera," she said.

I never thanked her. I just wrote the right answer down.

The banker walked her to the lobby. He held her hand. Then they parted.

"How long are you gonna stay married to this one?" I asked.

"Married? What are you talking about?" she asked and changed the subject. "What do you feel like doing tonight?"

"You have to do something every minute. Can't you stand still? You're going to have a heart attack by the time you're forty."

"I vote for the club."

It was as if she hadn't even heard me.

"It'll be fun. Melody is coming back tomorrow. We can't very well go with her."

"Your daughter's coming back tomorrow? I thought she was gone for the whole week."

"Nope tomorrow. I can't wait for you to see her."

Nikki wore a chocolate crochet mini-dress, and

she was twisting and turning, running her hands through the base of her collarbone length hair.

I wore a knee length skirt and long-sleeved shirt and stood over by the wall.

I was sorry she had nagged me into coming. I was so unused to the noise and the crowd and the pretense.

When Nikki came back over to where I was, I was even more depressed. I wished she'd stop standing near me. I felt impossibly flushed next to her one hundred and some change frames.Self-conscious about the size of my breasts, I covered them up by crossing my arms. Beside her, I was the consolation prize. Soon, another suitor swept her off for another whirl.

I watched her again. When she danced, she was free. Her bones are loose. Her knees would be cornflakes in ten years – shattered needing pins. Fellow after fellow came to dance with her. And she entertained them all.

Growing weary of the show, I made my way to the lady's room. While I washed my hands, Nikki appeared behind me.

"Hi Jean. Remember that? Hygiene." She laughed.

"I told you, I told you, I didn't want to come here."

"I'm sorry. I thought you'd enjoy it."

"What is there to enjoy?"

"I thought you'd like to see some of the nightlife here."

"You know there's a part of the body besides your pelvis. I hope you're not going to call any of those men. Think about your child."

"What does Melody have to do with anything?"

"All you care about is yourself. Every man you see you throw yourself at."

"What?"

"You heard me."

"What are you talking about?"

"You have no self-respect," I told her.

"Self-respect about what?"

"Nothing. Forget it."

"No, what do you mean?" She was tearing up. A couple of other audacious women walked by us with their ribs high and open.

I made a move to leave and she grabbed my shirt. "You're the one thing I knew was on my side. Wherever I went, I would get your letters."

"You don't need me, Nikki. You always do fine on your own."

"We grew up together."

"That was a long time ago," I told her. Then I walked away. I went out the door, then outside, and waited by her car.

Nikki's mother had episodes, gaps of time when she wouldn't leave her bed. Or comb her hair or eat. Her mother passed away five months after my father died. My father died of undiagnosed diabetes. Her mother swallowed a handful of pills. It was a hard junior year.

I don't know why I'd been so brittle to Nikki since I'd arrived. It was an equal mystery why I had exploded at her that night. I'd been looking forward to seeing her for so long.

I laid awake in the foldout pretending that none of it happened. Pretending that I'm back at home with my mom, and I hadn't even visited.

Deeper into the night, I overhead the following:

"You don't seem to have much in common," he said. It was the man from her shower.

"We grew up in the same town," Nikki said. "Who keeps up with those people?"

"Maybe we shouldn't have gone out. Maybe you should forget about her."

"We were best friends."

"That was how many years ago, Nikki?"

Nikki every few months sent me updated pictures of her daughter. Melody looked like a little boy though she had inherited her mother's heart-shaped face, pouty lower lip, and a nose that flipped up. Melody didn't have Nikki's swan neck. At least, not yet she didn't. Nikki's ex-mother-in-law lived in a big fancy brick house with a long lane leading up to it. The woman opened the door wearing matching slacks and a shirt, sort of soft blue green. She smiled warmly at Nikki and told her that Melody would be right out. Soon a little tomboy girl in sweats and a tee shirt emerged and gave Nikki the biggest hug I'd ever seen.

On the way back to Nikki's place, mother and daughter talked seemingly without taking a breath. Whenever they tried to include me, the conversation deflated.

Later in Nikki's apartment, Melody gave another meaningful hug to her mother, saying how happy she was to be home. Nikki went into the kitchen, and Melody eyed me, waiting for me to make the first move. I didn't.

Nikki had been treating me all along, but this was such an expensive restaurant. I don't know why she picked it with her dancer's salary and her daughter in tow.

I scanned the menu for something cheap. Soup was cheap, but hardly filling. I thought of ordering extra bread.

"Order whatever you like," Nikki said, reading my mind.

I now looked at the entrees. I settled on shrimp.

The tall, thin, waiter poured water with a dazzling smile, and his blue eyes settled on Nikki.

"Thank you, Claude," she said.

"It's Dwayne," the waiter said, gesturing to his nameplate. Nikki just smiled.

How did she do it? Make all these stupid gaffs and have people think she's so cute. Was it that face? That pleasant face. I wish I was like her. So pleasant. I realized I was hunched up, crabby.

He took my order functionally. He lingered on Nikki's. Milking each morsel for more conversations about the vegetarian dish she ordered.

"How long have you been a vegetarian?" he asked her.

"Since 1997. I had my last cheeseburger from a little square plastic box."

"I knew you were a vegetarian. Some people you can just tell."

I rolled my eyes. Didn't he see her child? Wouldn't that dissuade his overtures? This man looked all of twenty-two years old. What was wrong with him?

Throughout the meal, I had to endure her daughter giving me the stink eye and the waiter's outrageous flirtations.

"Why don't you tell me more about that guy?" Nikki asked.

"What guy?" I asked.

"The guy you were talking about from the internet."

"How do you meet guys off the internet?" Melody asked.

"I see him once a week. He's only available on Saturday," I said.

"One day a week?" Melody asked.

"He's an engineer. He travels a lot."

"I thought that was a nine-to-five type thing. You sit in an office and engineer," Nikki said.

"He travels a lot," I said.

"Probably to see his other girlfriend,"Melody said. Again, I noted the petulance in her voice, but there was nothing I did about it.

In my last morning at Nikki's, I eavesdropped on the following:

Melody scowled. "She's not like your other friends. She didn't bring me a present."

"That's not why you like someone, Sweetheart," Nikki said.

"It helps," Melody said.

Nikki put the Eggos in the toaster and gave Melody's pig-tails a quick brushing while she waited for the pop.

"Why is she going to sleep so early?"

"Some people go to sleep early," Nikki said.

"Not grown people. Plus, she wears granny clothes to bed."

"This is a free country, Melody."

"Ma, and how come she has Eggos every day. You won't let me eat the same thing every morning."

"She's an adult, Melody."

"She's not an adult. You told me she still lives with her ma."

"She loves her ma. There's nothing wrong with that."

"I love you, Ma, but when I turn eighteen, I'm out of here."

During my last moments in Minnesota, Nikki exited Route 35 and followed the twenty signs that lead to the airport.

She entered the short-term parking lot and paranoia struck me. What if I missed the plane? I didn't want to pay for a ticket exchange. I had less than an hour before boarding.

Nikki's eyes took in the panorama. "Now, where is the parking space?"

I frowned. "You can drop me off."

"Okay," Melody said.

"Melody." Nikki called her name as close to stern as I'd ever heard her.

Melody stamped her feet on the car's floor and turned away.

When Nikki found a spot, we all got out. I handed the ticket to Nikki, and Nikki looked it over noting the gate and letter number. She took my bag in one hand and Melody's hand in the other.

Nikki led the way with her sculpted shoulders back. We reached the plane as it was boarding.

The attendant pointed at me. "I need to see her ID."

"She needs your driver's license," Melody said to me.

Nikki went into my wallet and dug it out.

"Will you be helping her on board?" The stewardess asked.

"No, we're staying here," Melody said.

Both of them went to write out little ID cards. I was frozen, unable to help.

Nikki tied each bag with a bright green ribbon. She handed them to the attendant. Then there was a moment. A real moment, it seemed like just Nikki and I were the only two people on the tarmac. Or the world.

I looked into her warm, brown eyes. The corners of Nikki's lips twisting into little curlicues as she said, "Goodbye, Jean."

Before when I thought of our childhood, I thought of greenness and gladness − roller skating in the cemetery and paying single admission but seeing triple features at the Sameric. Because of this trip, it was harder to recall these things.

The next morning, there was no communication. No card, no call. I offered her nothing the following days, and weeks. Nikki was only to assume that I had made it home alright with my mother waiting at the airport gate.

I never contacted her again. I never checked to see if she was happy or not, or if she was still seeing that shirtless Latin, or if things got going with Dwayne or Claude (now I confused the name), or if she ever got that loan, or opened that studio, or if Melody was still into soccer, or street drugs. I never called, just to say hi.

Just the other day, I pictured Nikki standing there just out from the shower naked, only reaching for a towel when she saw me. I didn't know why that image occurred to me. Maybe, it was best that she stayed in her portion of the country. And I stayed in mine. I did wonder if she ever stared out the window thinking what happened to her best friend. Or was she over me—Did she go through the stages of loss? The anger, the denial. Anger, bargaining, anger, dancing. Acceptance.

Now all I had left of our friendship is the Kodak paper that pulsed bright greens, vivid reds, sunshiny yellows, and our skin warm brown like bread just from the oven.

From each faded picture, I couldn't help but think of that piece-of-clay word, friend. Last night, I even stayed up late. I thought of it, her, as I watched the stars hanging, clustering, and burning.

Life as a Cliché

So trite, my boss, stereotypically balding, puts his hands on my shoulder while I was processing words instead of word processing. Are you some kind of writer? he asks. When I don't answer, his hands move up to play with my earrings, which dangle parallel to my cheekbones. Can you work late tonight? He wants to know.

So, I had to fuck him. Certainly, I can't support myself off my anemic symbolism, my flabby free verse. I need to keep my clerical skills employed.

So the next morning, during dictation, in my embroidered white blouse, crisp to the point of snapping, I remain unaltered. Our eyes meet: his loaded with metaphor; mine without the least suggestion of allusion.

The Bard of Frogtown

Like most writers I am full of shit.

Sometimes I look at the piles and piles of half started prose and think, "Got a match?"

And then, I think, I'll write a poem. Poems save paper.

So all of a sudden I am a poet. Yet, I still have nothing to say.

Write, writer, write! Goddamn it, write you fucking idiot. Asshole, hole in the ass. Craphead. Son of a bitch!

Hey!

What?

Don't get personal.

By the way, my real father, yes, the one I have never seen in my life, is a goddamn poet. My mother still gets an occasional sestina through the mail from his as yet to be published chapbook entitled, *The Part of Me that No OneKnows*.

Tell me about it.

Yet as a poet, I just don't feel like I am any good.

When I was younger I used to read my stuff with a sense of accomplishment. Now I just cringe. After work I come home and try to get busy on something gold and it turns on trite, banal, and unkempt.

Children are natural artists then they get old and they dry up. I am 19 now. And as I keep saying I have nothing to say.

I've lived with Debra for the past four years.

When I left home it was like a funeral except no one had died. I was so sad. I cried once I hit the main drag.

Big tears, buckets of them.

I was fifteen, when Debra and I found our own place.

We moved from a little town to a big city. From West to East while still staying North. We live in rough and tumble Frogtown. In Frogtown, us people sell crafts, they line the drags with their handufactured baskets, pottery, metal works, and textiles.

She is a little bit older than me and helped me out a great deal. Not just with the security deposit but she listen to me hash out about my childhood. Long nights we spent therapeutically bottle and blunt passing till I got it all out, the words. I realized now that not only do I hate my stepfather, but I also resent my younger brother, and that my mother is a continual source of frustration.

With all that memesized and catharsis size, I should crack open like an egg. I should have plenty to write about. I should look at a blank piece of paper and fill it.

I wash airplanes for a living.

Somebody has to.

I wake up at five in the AM and go down to the airport and scrub the thick plastic windows with a long handled brush. I have always loved planes, always dreamed of floating above things. Tempting God with man-made angel wings.

When I got home this afternoon, Debra was in broken-in jeans, a teal tee shirt and the familiar fawn colored leather jacket. She wears all of this indoors because we have limited heat. Sometimes the walls get frost-covered.

Still, Debra is a diligent writer. She does songs. I walk in and she is holding the guitar pick between her teeth as she scribbles notes on a page. She flicks her head back and winks at me. She is a winker. Always winking, and I think just who in the hell wears the pants in this relationship.

She does.

Debra loves bits of clutter: Books and papers and hankies that she blew her nose on. I can't stand it.

Often I just want to tidy up but dare I take liberties with her, her, her—well, I suppose genius is as good a word as any.

But perhaps it's still not the right one.

A few months ago, Debra sold one of her songs to a big deal Cosmopolitan company. She got 500 dollars outright. We had steak for a week. That's the problem with being a Zoe and dealing with the Cosmos everything you sell is sold outright and haven't us Blacks given enough away.

They have stolen our land, our women, now our music.

The name of the song was, "A White Sleeve of Moonlight." And when Debra sang it felt Black. It was textual and lilting yet bodacious as cowboys. She used steel strings instead of the Cosmopolitan twinkling of a piano. I heard the Cosmo version on the radio and I almost kept passing the dial. It was a totally different song, and a corny one at that.

Oh Debra... She was the sanctuary from my problems I forgot she had so many of her own. She was like a regular Zoe with a family tree that tangled at the root. I could never get it straight but I knew she was the half-sister of the dead Rice Street Man. The Rice Street Man that my brother, Solly, was so enamored with. The Rice Street Man that smelled worse than his dog. And as if that weren't bad enough, quite a few of Debra's short on dollars, long in the tooth relatives used to stay over temporarily for months and months. And poor little Deb was treated like she was invisible. She was forced into disappearing to create a room.

She used to have to give up her bedroom and sleep on the couch. It was then that she learned to play that funky old guitar that she'd found in a dumpster. At night while all the live-ins where raising Hell she'd mouth the words, practice fingering, playing without sound. Just another blond haired girl, in a country that over flowed with them. So unprettied up, you could take her for granted. I have never seen her in a dress but then again she's never seen me in one either. I like to use her life in my writing even more than I like to use my life in my writing.

Writers are the worst type of people God ever put on this earth. They note the way the dirt falls on a casket of a dear friend because they know they can use it later.

It is always my writing, my writing, my writing. The whole fucking world revolves around my writing.

I want to write a poem.

Lovers make the worst critics, so why do I always ask my Debra?

I show her my words few and she says, "I don't know it sort of sticks in my throat."

I snatch the paper back from her and tell her that she was supposed to fucking read it not fucking eat it.

She laughs at me. She laughs at me. She throws her lovable head back and laughs at me.

I read my work aloud:

Salt without bread.

Thorns on a cactus.

Buddy Holly, I miss you.

Why didn't you go Greyhound?

I smile, puffing my chest out. Sure, it needs some revision but it's not all bad. The images are clear and concrete. The sound and rhythm may need some spit and polish.

All right, it sucks.

It bites the big wiener.

But at least it has punctuation and it does not employ the lowercase "i".

I want to be Langston Hughes.

Enough of these meditations. These scream fests on the mysteries of freedom, love, and hate.

I want to be remembered.

I know I am not a great writer I am only a great re writer. Half the time there is nothing pithy in the first draft. Half the time I don't know where it's going at all. I don't have a style or tone that I wish to effect. I feel like screaming at myself where is my theme?

Where is my message? Why am writing this poem in the first place.

I will switch back to prose.

Inside every fiction writer there is a failed poet.

Metaphors, like my heart is dry like a big red balloon, are inflated but then I think all right so where do I go from there?

I break for supper. Debra fixed homemade pizza pie with marmot meat and shrooms as topping. I down a few pizza slices and drop the crust. She's not a bad cook, but I'm a little better, I measure, I do not guestamate so much.

She has a great smile, nothing but teeth. Big teeth and squinchy eyes. I enjoy this time a couple of low rent artists eating pizza off a white plate with blue trim. She asks me about the planes and I tell her quite recently they had entrusted me with an unbelievable amount of keys.

"How many is too many to believe?"

"37."

"Unbelievable," she winks at me. "Now don't fly off with the place."

I stand and she makes a grab for my butt, smiling, "Off to do more writing?" she asked.

"That's a good question," I answer.

After our meal she washes the dishes and I take my compositions to the bedroom.

In this next expanse of time, I had done everything to write. I drew a bath, drank some murk, splashed cold water in my ears, danced the bop, the bump, the butterfly, the electric slide, the four corners, the icky shuffle, the mashed potato, the shingling, the worm. I felt refreshed, but still no words.

So I light up and dream, I was making love to Debra only she has thick black hair and the wind blows and exposes her blond roots. Her eyeliner ran down her cheeks like fast graffiti. Those long full breasts had shrunk to teacups.

I dream of white food as symbolism. Rice pudding and glazed doughnuts.

SPACE. Time and space. Time sitting, smoking in the numb silence, watching the snow, as if it were doing something wild, like disappearing instead of the same old same old. I press my face against the pane and gaze at the wide, white city below.

Winter. Heavy snowstorms at the floodgates bringing up a whirlpool of memories. Snowing as marvelous as sugar — pink and white candy-coated Christmas.

Debra, her bland blue eyes told of a fairy tale of cabbage and rye toast. Toy soldiers. Debra belting a rendition of "White Christmas". I start singing along real low and soft you'd have to read my kisser to tell.

Wilting.

The soundtrack mixes over and over.

"Are you gonna share or is a contact high all that I can hope for?" is the question that wakes me.

Debra stands by the doorway, 25 years old, and wasting her time on me. I'm just an adult child still so full of dream. Unable to achieve any synthesis. I roll an herb her way.

Sometimes it's better not to force it I think as my ram road is in her and I'm frictioning her. Sometimes it's better to distill in the hope of further cross fertilization.

I do have a beginning of something:
Snow like sweat
or smoke, like mercury,
rising above itself
in a cloud.

Choice

My days were chaotic and flipped. It wasn't until 9pm when the kids were good asleep that I got around to drinking coffee and reading the morning newspaper. The Wednesday paper was thick with advertisements and a huge food spread. I was at the Metro section when the phone rang. It was the woman from the agency. She asked after Brittany and then Alicia.

She had my youngest daughter's name wrong. I corrected her. "Ashley's fine too."

"Oh, I'm sorry; I meant that." I heard the shifting of papers. "How are you?"

"I'm fine. How are you?" I asked her.

"I'm fine."

"Good."

"Good."

Next, there was deep blue silence. I sipped my coffee and glanced at the end of section B, the obituary page.

"She's had another, Miss Phillips. Another girl. It was born two days ago. It had all ten fingers and all ten toes."

From the living room, I eyed the door to the girls' room and my eyes then lowered. "How did she get pregnant again? I thought she was in jail."

"She is."

"She's in jail and pregnant?" I asked.

"She gave birth. I really hate calling you. I hate telling you this."

"How could you let that happen?"

"I'm really the middle man," she explained.

"I can't take on another child," I told her.

"You don't have to decide this minute. Why don't I call you in a few days?"

"Where is she now?"

"In jail."

"No, the baby."

"The facility has temporary housing for –"

A chill went through me. "That's a sin. The baby is in custody?"

"Miss Phillips, this is the way things work."

"How could you let this happen?"

"Please, I almost didn't call, but I thought you should know. Miss Phillips, I'm giving you too much at once. I'll call you back in a few days."

"Her tubes should be cut, and they should be fried," my sister told me.

"The child is already here."

"Then let Steven Spielberg adopt it. He likes our people. He's a millionaire. You are a secretary barely making 30 a year. He has an estate. You have a lousy apartment."

My sister was in finance and dapper like a cat with large made-up eyes and a new outfit every week. She always railed me about my cramped 700 square foot apartment. Helen was self-oriented, so naked in her hedonism, so singular, so opinionated. But there are advantages of a deadbeat. She sat as I unpacked the groceries and sat as I put away the groceries and sat as I began making super. I was making a steak sandwich just like the sub shops did with all the fixings: tomatoes and peppers and fried onions and grease. I placed the frozen meat portions in the pan.

I worked in a gray building filing papers. We looked alike, my adoptive children and I; the rich mocha and cocoa hues of my skin matched theirs. They look like childhood pictures of myself and my sister with our wide brimmed noses, rust colored plaits, and other genetic trademarks.

Four could live as cheaply as three right? Right? What's another pair of school shoes, more money for milk, another college fund? I should take in that child. I have to.

I kept my hair short, but I straightened it. I wear slacks most days, not skirts because I don't have the time to fuss with leg shaving and panty hose.

I haven't had a date in two years, but it's not my children's fault. I never dated much before them.

"Stop trying to save the whole goddamn world."

"Do you have to put it like that, Helen?"

"What, you want to be like everyone else? So PC that I'm not saying anything. Look, I voted in the last election. I serve on juries. I pay taxes on time. I've even given the Red Cross a whole freaking fracking pint of my blood. I'm a good person."

"They aren't the kind of girls where a lot of strangers would coo over. I don't think Steven Spielberg is the answer," I said. Brittany came addicted: underweight, about as heavy as a shadow, shaking, ashy complexioned. I sat up with her many a night trying to undo what had been done to her while she lived in someone else's womb. I didn't choose to have Ashley one year later. If it was up to me, I would have spaced them in a three years span. I got Ashley at two weeks and even then, she looked stunted and underdeveloped.

So, now six years later, there's an addition.

Ashley has trouble sleeping. What would it be with a crying baby in the house?

"Why didn't this woman have an abortion?" Helen asked. "At least with an abortion, you know it's over this. Shit, doesn't it bother her not knowing what happened to this little girl?"

Babies are so easy to love. They are so small and helpless looking and have limited emotional range: they laugh and cry easily and are easily entertained with animal quilts and balloons and monotonous music.

What would a boy be like? But it's already a girl.

I could recite twinkle, twinkle little star to her.

"I can't leave her in there," I said in a clear defeated voice.

"Why not? She's not yours. You keep messing around and you're going to be like those people on *20/20*." Helen said with dull bluntness. "They got a kid from each country. Shit. It's not your problem. Have them call up one of those Scientologists. Are you crying?"

"No, I'm just slicing onions."

Helen got up and took the knife from my hands. She began chopping, without tears or remorse.

"Jesus is sitting around the table with the apostles and he asks Paul, "Paul, what do you bring?" Paul says, "Sorry, Jesus, I forgot." Then Jesus turns to John and asks John, "What did you bring?" And John says, "I'm sorry, I didn't bring anything." So Jesus says, "Okay, apostles, you have done this to me time and time again: This is your last supper."

The girls laughed. The joke was a little long for the pay off, but I was grateful that Helen had told a clean joke.

"You see, even Jesus had His limits," she said, winking at me.

Now, I got it. I never figured my sister as a wit.

The sandwiches had come out well. The bread was juicy with beef grease.

"T-t-tell us another joke, Aunt Helen," Brittany said. She had a stuttering problem when she got overexcited.

Helen basked it the attention. She leaned back and thought hard.

The phone rang. I went to pick it up.

"Miss Philips?" The voice on the other end was the agency woman.

"You said you would give me a few days," I reminded her.

"Mommy, who is it?" Brittany asked me.

I put my hands to my lips gesturing for her to shhh.

"Is it --" Helen began but stopped herself. She nodded knowingly, and her eyes burned into me.

"Miss Phillips, I know, but I really want to move on this. We can arrange to have to have you take the child –"

"I'm not going to do it. Find another home for her." I kept a hard face as if she could see it through the receiver.

"W-w-who's h-her, Mommy?" Brittany asked.

"Brittany, be quiet," Helen said and gave me the thumbs up.

"Are you sure you don't need more time to think about it?" the agency lady asked me.

"Who's Mommy talking to?" Ashley asked.

"I can't," I told the lady. "Helen, could you take the girls into the next room?"

Helen took their hands and led them away looking back at me, saying 'you're doing the right thing'.

"You can name this one," the social worker told me. This dangled like a charm. Adoptive mother don't getto make many decisions. My mind went heavy for amoment. I did hate the names Brittany and Ashley. I know of no famous women in history with these soulless, polo club names. I would like to name a daughter after my great-grandmother Bessie or maybe even something afrocentric.

"Miss Phillips —"

I hung up the phone before I had a chance to change my answer to yes.

Something in Between

In a sports bra worn thin by use and sweats that once tight hung were now loose, Jennifer ran five miles before her morning class. It was her second favorite part of the day.

Her bare feet hit the unyielding pavement, shock waves assaulting her feet, ankles, knees, and back. Though the hurt felt good, she vowed that, when she hit 25, she'd stop this. By that time, she'd be totally grown, married, have children, and spending hours in front of an ironing board. She'd be too worried about how the table linens looked to indulge in a hobby as consuming as this.

In the meantime, it was pure bliss: running and running and running. Arms and legs churning. Body floating. Like a waterfall, like Niagara, pouring herself through the sunrise. When she got back to Powelton Street, she launched into one last burst of speed as she crossed the finish line, the entrance to her dorm.

Her suitemates were either at breakfast eating those horrible pancakes with disgusting syrup or they were asleep, lazing away the best part of the day.

Jennifer paused before keying into her room when she saw the following message scrawled on her magnetic message board: *Call your father. Security Badge #24.*

Jennifer's chest constricted. She turned and ran back down to the lobby. There, she saw one of them in navy slacks, gray shirt, and navy suit coat.

"Are you #24?" she asked.

She noticed the guard eying her up. She was about his height, but only a quarter of his size. He didn't run, he was too wide backed, too flat footed, too easily winded. Security guards didn't have to pass a physical. They just had to show up on time and try not to doze off during the long lulls of inaction. "I'm badge #24. You college students read very well."

"What's the matter with my father?" she asked.

"Call him."

"What's the matter with him?"

"Call your father," the uniformed man told her. "Why are you making problems? Just call your father."

"I just—" Jennifer began.

"Call your father." The man spoke over her, then opened up his logbook and made a notation.

Jennifer turned and walked back to the elevator, frowning. As difficult as this fat security guard was, he was like sweet potato pie compared to her father. Talking to her father was like crossing a mined bridge.

So she didn't call him.

She took a shower and got dressed for her first class, Nutrition. There she got her assignment back, her three-day diary of food intake. Her professor wrote back a simple question: Not eating much? A checkmark. During class, the prof touched on the Metropolitan Life Insurance weight charts. According to it, a healthy female between the ages of eighteen to twenty-two and her height should weigh between 120 and 130 pounds. And that was just for those who were considered to have a small frame. Those charts were wrong, she thought. She weighed a good 112 and she was looking to shave off another 5 or 10, just for good measure.

At 11:00am to 11:50am, she sat in Calculus class.

At noon, she had Intro to Lit.

Her father didn't like her attending college. He'd always said it was a waste of time, and she wasn't smart enough. He thought she ought to stay home with him and keep him company.

"A family should be close," he would say.

Jennifer's skin was brown. The perfect in between of her mother's lightness and her father's deep skin tone. Her father felt she should have been nearer to her mother's hue. He brought this up to her over and over again as if his criticism could make her different.

As a child, she was a fussy eater and very thin boned. By the time, she reached adolescence, she had put on weight due to a combination of puberty and adjusting to the loss of her mother.

"Come here, let me weigh you," her father teased her.

"You're going to be really big later on," he warned. "You're drinking milk?!" he had exclaimed. "You're eating potatoes and bread. No wonder your butt is so big." Her father was a visionary, into the Atkins Diet without even reading any of that doctor's book.

Her father was a thin, stringy man who always wore long sleeves even in the swelter of August. He was simultaneously proud and ashamed of his slim physique. Jennifer used to wish her father was more generous with his praise or his affection. Over the years, she had been so worn down she simply wished that he'd leave her alone.

A few weeks ago, she'd spent winter break with him, and he

badgered her daily. She was glad to escape to school. It wasn't due to her vast number of friends. She wanted to be a history major but she knew her father wouldn't approve of that. So she was undeclared, as an UND, she took foundation classes.

One more run in the low sun, the fading sun. She needed it to give here the strength to call. To punch the numbers.

"Hi, Daddy," she said.

"How come you never call?" he asked. She could imagine his jawbone jutting out in anger.

"I just called you Monday."

"You never call. I don't know what you're doing to keep you so busy."

"I'm calling you now."

"Well, it's about time."

"You didn't have to call security."

"You are supposed to call me everyday. That's why I called security. You were going to let this whole week pass weren't you?"

Jennifer didn't answer. She just felt the sweat in her palm make the phone hard to grip.

"I got your report card, Jennifer."

"They sent it home?"

"You shouldn't even be at the school."

"Daddy —"

"You're getting Cs. Cs."

"What?" she asked.

"That's all you got was Cs. Is that all you can do?!" he asked her.

Jennifer wondered whether he was holding the report in his hand or had he committed it to memory. She wanted to ask specifically what did she get in Freshman Comp, she thought she'd done well in that class. She'd gotten a B+ on her midterm.

His anger showed no signs of lifting. He was like a hot, flat iron moving back and forth over her.

Jennifer looked out through the window. Night wove its darkness even deeper. He yelled at her for a good five minutes before he let her go.

Her ears were ringing; her heart was pounding, thundering in her chest, yet she shed no tears. Her face was impassive. She had learned that much.

She wasn't really smart at all. What was she doing in college anyway? Maybe she should kill herself, she thought, but then recovered.

Jennifer's suitemates, Connie and Sara, were from Massapequa and Albany, respectively, they were used to tree lined streets and manicured lawns. So was Jennifer. She was from Binghamton.

That night they went to a party. There was nothing to eat, but plenty to drink. Kegs of icy beer.

He noticed her—a small, slender, brown, young woman biting her lower lip. Jennifer always had to be doing something. Moving somehow.

She wasn't the prettiest, but that night she did look among the most desirable to him. Despite their racial differences, he picked up on her availability. Though she wore a frozen smile she wore that never reached her eyes, she was at least smiling.

"Hey, Jane," he said to her.

"It's Jennifer."

"Sorry."

"You don't have to be sorry, you were close."

"I'm Trent. I'm in your Lit. class. I missed it today."

"How come?"

"I overslept. Did Professor Hass collect the journals?"

She nodded.

"I don't like short stories. I can't get into them," Trent said.

"The one that we did today wasn't bad," Jennifer said.

"What was it about?" he asked, stepping a little closer to her.

"I don't remember."

They laughed.

He drank his fourth can of the night.

She was still on her first. She didn't like consuming too many carbs.

"I see you running a lot," he said.

"I like to run," she said, "Do you run?"

"I hate it."

He was lean of body — fit, wiry muscles. Short like her father. "You must do something, Trent. You look fit."

"Me? I can't keep weight on."

"Lucky you," she said.

"What are you talking about? You have a beautiful body."

"I'm all right."

During sex with Trent in his dorm room, she wished she was running as the rain shone on the pavement. Why was she thinking of all of this when he was on top of her, giving her what he had in jolts, faster and faster?

The blood rushed swiftly to his face making it red as though he were angry. Veins in his forehead stood out thick and swollen, as if angry at her.

There's no dating in college. There is just coupling on bedrolls surrounded by unfolded laundry and milk crates.

After he climaxed, he pulled out and gave her a single kiss

on the lips. Then he rolled over and fell asleep. The condom was still on him, loose and filled with juice. He'd be out cold till about noon or maybe even 2pm. She got her things together and slipped out. She walked with the path highlighted by red security call boxes thinking how the first semester had been a dream, a kaleidoscope, a mesh of possibility. This second semester was shaping up to be reality.

The next morning, she was the only one up in her suite. She went into the bathroom. Connie's hot pink shag rug gave it a homey appeal. The other girls left their caddies filled with mascara, shadow, eyeliner, blush, and lipstick. The digital scale, wedged in between the sink and the toilet, was Jennifer's donation to this space.

Jennifer stood on it. She was down a half a pound from the previous day. She felt proud. This was the happiest part of her day.

Sweet Thang

I can travel through time; sometimes it's voluntary; sometimes it's not. Just the other night, I saw a movie with these white people with dark hair -- I think they were Italian. In this film, there was a funeral scene where the main character jumped in after the coffin was lowered the six feet into the ground, and all of a sudden I was at that day. My reality, though, had black people all dressed in black and only a smattering of whites from the nursing program she was in. She left behind a son. She had named him Tracy John Upshaw.

She was Karyn. I knew her as Auntie; she was Daddy's little sis.

I recall everything annoyed me that day. I was watching Auntie Karyn in her coffin, and I knew Auntie Karyn was watching me. At the gravesite, the Reverend Whitaker, who wore his hair in a Caesar, led us away, saying, "There's nothing we can do now."

I didn't want to be ushered to the side, and I hated those words: "There is nothing we can do now." Especially the word "nothing." There had to be something—something that would bring her back.

Reverend Whitaker had his arm bracing, then moving, me. My legs felt like they might fold. Off by the limo, other relatives were sobbing in one big huddled mass.

The last look at Auntie made my chest hurt. I was only nine, but I felt like I was having a heart attack. Auntie had always been fair, but her face was now whiter, glittering, and waxen. Each hope, every dream, every prayer was lost, gone. Her large penny-colored eyes were closed forever.

Back at the house, my nuclear-and-beyond family gathered, and Otis Redding was playing on the stereo, singing that Fa Fa Fafafafa sad song. There was a lot of chicken. Fried, braised, broiled, roasted in a pan, chicken pot pie. So much damn food—nine trays of potato salad. Distant relations ate heartily, even sloppily, macaroni salad sliding off their spoons onto their chins.

Tracy John was asleep during most of that day. He was passed from arm to arm. Everyone wanted to hold the precious one; he was like a hot potato in reverse. Family and friends didn't leave till it was night. Then it really sank in—I'll never see her again.

"I just want to know why," I sobbed in my open hands.

Daddy's usual husky/tender voice offered no explanation. He just held me while I pulled myself together again. Though he didn't sob that day, neither in public nor just with me, I realized that he wasn't whole. Like the rest of us who loved her, he would have a hole in the heart that wouldn't go away.

With the sun now down, sorrow solidified with the moon. My head felt lighter. My heart was heavier.

Around midnight, Uncle O's car broke down by the airport. He said the engine died. Daddy took jumper cables and my older brother, Horace, to Island Avenue to rescue him.

That night my eyes were propped open by an unknown force. I wished Daddy had taken me instead of Horace. Maybe working a jack or holding a flashlight could have gotten my mind off my heart and the pain that it felt.

Gammy had Tracy John for the rest of the week, and I thought she was going to keep him. The following week, he was with us; mid-week, Gammy took him back. Then that Friday, I was over Uncle O's apartment, and Tracy John was there.

By the end of the month, he was at our house, and I guessed that Tracy John was going to stay with us forever, which back then wasn't a problem. He was small and playful with Daddy, Ma, and my two brothers, Horace and Leo. And he stayed out of my way. I think something changed when he was in the first grade, but I'm not sure. Maybe the change was in me, for it has taken me this long to discover that Tracy John ruled. For example, within a week of Tracy John moving into our home for good, I lost my room.

After Ma told me, I screamed, "What?!"

Daddy backed her up by repeating what they'd decided.

"No, no," I pleaded. "Let him move in with Leo."

"Leo is moving in with you, Charmaine," Ma said.

"But he's a boy. I can't live with a boy."

"Boy, girl, don't make no matter." Daddy waved me away. "We're all family."

I turned to Ma. "I don't have any friends who share a room with their brothers."

"Then you don't have any friends who share a room with their brothers," Daddy said. "That doesn't mean nothing. You and your brother will live together. That's how they do it in the country."

"What country?" I asked.

Daddy shot me a look that told me it was in my best interest not to seek any more answers. I didn't argue with Daddy; for you see, even at the age of nine, I was pro-life —my own.

Inside, I was mad. How could they do a thing like that to me? How did Tracy John get his own room? Tracy John could have stayed with Leo, or Horace for that matter. Tracy John wouldn't even know the difference.

As worried as I was back then, now, at fourteen, things have reached crisis proportions. I'd calmed down, but each day I learned it was all about His Highness. The precious one, Tracy John Upshaw.

Just last month, Tracy John almost cost Daddy sixty dollars for a pair of glasses that he didn't need. Ma had taken him to get his eyes examined for the start of the school year. Tracy John had been reading ever since he was three-and-a-half, so he knew his letters very well. The doctor discerned that Tracy John should wear a strong prescription because he'd read all but the two top lines wrong. Ma escorted him to the eyeglass shop. Over the next two hours, Tracy John tried on children's frames. He didn't like one.

When they came home, Tracy John pointed at me and said, "I want glasses like her."

Her? Her! It's only like I lived in the same house with him. He'd known me his whole life. I wasn't a "her" to be pointed at like some stranger on the street. I was only his blood relative: Charmaine. He could have called me that, or Maine, like everyone else.

"You tried on glasses like that, Honey," Ma said to him, with patience and understanding.

"I want her glasses," Tracy John repeated as if he was going to grab them right from my face.

The next day Ma, pixie-faced Tracy John, and I went all the way downtown to another eyeglass store. This time Tracy John spent another two hours trying on forty-seven pairs of frames. I was about to blow my stack hearing Ma alternate between, "Do you like this one, Sugar?" and, "How about this, Pumpkin?" Even the salesclerk was in on the act, calling him, "Peanut". They patted him on the head after fitting each frame around his ears. It was outrageous.

The other patrons smiled and cooed at him, and over time they formed a small circle about him. In the end, Tracy John settled on a pair of glasses that looked nothing like my octagon-shaped frames. His choice was small, black wire glasses that looked Ben Franklin-ish.

The shop promised to put in a rush job on account of the doctor's report saying Tracy John was half-blind. Ma left a ten-dollar deposit, leaving a balance of over fifty. We took the 13 trolley back to our home in Dardon. No sooner were we on the streetcar than Tracy John tugged at Ma's arm and said, "I don't want glasses. I see twenty."

Ma gave him a quizzical look.

He was insistent. "I see twenty."

We got off at the next stop and caught the other trolley going back to Center City. Back at the eye doctor, it was conclusive. In fact, Tracy John did see twenty. Twenty-twenty.

What had Tracy John done the previous day? Just made up letters like some damn fool. Later, Ma told Daddy, and he just chuckled at it.

Further into the evening, Daddy was in the living room, Tracy John cuddled in his lap. He sneaked a sip of his beer. This kid was too much. Daddy encouraged him. Habitually, Daddy would tell him to run into the kitchen and tell Ma a bad word. Tracy John would run into the kitchen and say, "Unc told me to say bullshit". And Daddy would laugh at Ma's fit. This left me to wonder—would Tracy John get away with all this mayhem if he weren't walking around with Auntie Karyn's face?

As I watched this *Godfather* imitation and reflected on gangsters and spoiled brats, the phone rang. Ma told me it was for me.

I walked to the phone, wishing I had my own phone in my own room, so that people wouldn't listen like stowaways to my conversation. I wanted a king-sized bed with a heavy velvet canopy where I could talk the day away. Instead I had the phone stretched into the bathroom.

I closed the door and sat on the lidded toilet seat. I was on the phone only ten minutes—I was talking to my best friend, Millicent, about that new boy at school who was the son of a surgeon, Demetrius McGee.

"Did you see him in that blue sweater, Millicent? He has to be the best-looking guy ever. He looks like a Greek god. An African-Greek god," I said.

"Oh, Demetrius!" Leo and Tracy John mock-swooned in unison behind the door.

I was endlessly heckled. They just didn't understand when I was talking about something important.

"Excuse me, Millicent," I said into the phone and then put it to the side. I opened the bathroom door to them.

"Will you two get out of here?!"

They laughed all over themselves, especially Tracy John with his sickeningly-sweet, squinched-up face.

"Shoe y'all," I told them, and chased them back into the living room.

As soon as I was back on the phone, my mother told me to get off, complaining about message units.

"Millicent, I gotta go." I hung up.

That was the last straw: I had to have my own room! I

wanted my own room, so I could play my own music (my Roberta Flacks and Al Greens). I needed privacy. Our house was worse than Watergate; filled with bugs, and not the kind that you could spray with Raid. This was a slow night; usually I couldn't even get the bathroom to myself when I was talking on the phone. There was no place to get away from everyone. I'd go in one room and Leo and Tracy John would be in there. In another, Horace would have a girl or his recruiter over; he was about to go to basic training. I'd go downstairs, and Daddy and his pinochle friends would be there. Ma would be in the kitchen, running the faucet, clattering the pots and pans or silverware, and I would try to slip away before she had a chance to see her and ask me to help her stir butter into the beans or mix the gravy or mashed potatoes.

Dejected, I went to my half of the room. Though Leo wasn't as bad as a proverbial jailhouse Bubba, this had to be worse than a jail cell. Leo kept his side of the room neat. He always picked up after himself and had the foot locker organized well. I thought of that copycat *Godfather* movie and turned the lights off, drawing the curtains, shutting out the streetlight. I was cold. It was going to be a hard winter. Soon I'd have to have to sleep with my socks on.

I couldn't sleep, so I thought about her.

Usually, it worked the other way: I'd wake in the night thinking of her. I lifted my head from the pillow, so I could hear. I waited, waiting in the nothingness of three a.m.—or maybe four. The quick shuffle. The hiss of the water pot. She'd be downstairs with her nurse books.

Auntie Karyn.

It's a funny thing; just when I thought it was under control, that's when it would hit me. Maybe it wasn't about the movie.

Maybe it was because Horace was due to ship out in about a week. A June graduate of Dardon Senior High, Horace signed up for the service after a long summer of Daddy badgering him: "No son of mine is living in this house and not working." It wasn't like 'Nam was still going on, but it did mean our family would once again be broken up.

Time.

The occasional mail came with an occasional phone call from people who I supposed had been on Mars and had no idea she'd been killed. They'd want to know details—as if to recall the details weren't painful for us to recount. Daddy would handle it by providing curt commentary:

"She died."

"She was twenty-four."

"Yeah."

"Then he shot himself."

"Yeah, he should have done that first."

"Yeah, it's that kind of world."

People generally said the same thing when they learned of her passing. They said she was so nice/so pretty/it was such a shame. Five years after her death, I am still trying to make sense of it. And I, at fourteen, don't think I ever will.

Jaclyn

She tried another doctor that day. Another plastic surgeon.

She stood before the bathroom mirror in a creamy cardigan and a long-pleated skirt; she knew the place by heart. The scar that snaked across her lower left jaw, its ugliness. She shined up her image and applied the therapeutic mixture, the wheat germ oil and the chamomile and marigold extract, rubbing it in aggressively. Dot it on, and then grind it in. Again. She looked at it closely for any improvement. Though it was months since the attack, she hadn't gained any objectivity. It was 2:40 in the afternoon; the appointment was at 4pm.

Her husband, Tracy stole up behind her, grabbing her ass, kissing her, sloppy as a used Kleenex. He squeezed her and kissed her some more. He wasn't mindful of her scar or her meticulous painting of it. His lips were greasy from the ointment as he said, "Sorry, I'm late. It was a shit getting out of work today. You ready?"

She gathered up all the crushed vitamins, plants, and sprouts in her cosmetic pail and nodded. They went out to his Camray, which was nothing for him but everything to her. She was dazzled by the brightness of the sky overhead. Pale blue and spotted with cotton. She hadn't been outside all week. Tracy opened the door for her, guiding her into the passenger side.

"I hope this doctor's better than the last one. Man that last one was right out of Doctor Frankenstein." Tracy said. "What's that crazy thing he wanted you to try?"

"Isologen," she said.

"That's it yeah, yeah—isolgen. That's science fiction. That doctor's motherfucking loco. He was going to take skin cells from behind your ear and grow them in the lab overnight then inject it back into the scar like that is supposed to work. That's white people for you. They go for all that motherfucking cloning and motherfucking body part swapping. They don't like to leave nothing where it's supposed to be. It's like all that in vitro shit. They take the egg from one woman and put it in another − yuck!"

Tracy still had his head going from side to side grooving to MJ's magical ending. His urging us all to get with that man in the mirror.

"That is some song, Peach… I don't think he really touched those boys."

"I don't think he's ever had plastic surgery." Jaclyn said as they rounded into the parking lot.

Tracy chuckled at that. They stood in front of the three-story red brick building trying to orient them. Jaclyn showed him the letter again and they went up to suite 301. They signed in and were shown to a virgin pink lobby filled with middle-aged white women with smile lines. Jaclyn's heart sank; she really wanted to see people who looked like her.

"Ain't they got a *Sports Illustrated?*" Tracy asked, shuffling through the pile of women's magazines. The *Vogues*, the *Elles*, the *Marie Claires*. "They ain't got no *Jet* neither. They ain't got nothing for the Black man."

He grabbed one of the breast augmentation brochures. You know the one where it said "as we age our breasts become longer and lower." Tracy opened it up to see the perky after picture and exclaimed, "Lord Almighty!"

The patrons' expressions didn't unfrown.

Jaclyn looked through the stacks until she found a *Newsweek* with the latest school shootings on the cover. She handed this to Tracy to keep him occupied.

Soon her name was called. "Jaclyn Upshaw."

She sat there and let her whole life flash before her eyes.

"Jaclyn Upshaw."

Tracy poked her. "That's you, Peach."

She gave a weak in the knees walk following the brown haired, freckled-faced nurse who was ample but had a switch to her walk. She sat Jaclyn on a metal table with sheet paper covering.

Then the doctor came in. He was not tall or short but had rimless glasses. He shot her rimless glances. "Now, Miss," he began and glanced at the chart. "I'm sorry, Mrs. Upshaw. So you're married…" He looked her up and down. "Recently?"

"Five years ago."

"That's a long time for someone as young as yourself. You are?" he flipped the folder open and squinted at the print.

"I'm 24." She answered with a sinking heart.

"Well, let's take a look."

She turned to the light. He held her chin. Her copper brown face burned. The clock ticked louder as a silence filled the room.

He left out a breath and began "Now, you are Black."

Space. Was that a question?

"Black skin is a very, very particular type of skin." He continued. "Very sensitive. It scars easily."

Especially when a knife was used on it, Jaclyn thought to herself.

"If we do dermabrasion which is a grinding of the top layers. Now, it might lead to hyperpigmentation. If we do an incision, which is to cut the scar out it will lead to hyperpigmentation. So you see, Mrs. Upshaw, between the hyper and the hypo, you are between a rock and a hard place. I would say forget about this scar. Pour yourself into your work. What is it that you do for a living?"

"I used to teach music."

"What type of music?"

"K through 12."

"Do you have kids of your own?"

"No."

"Then pour yourself into your husband."

Jaclyn moved back from the light.

"Forget about this minor imperfection." The doctor said, "You don't need to be sucked in by this lookist society. You don't need to bother yourself worrying about a scar as small and insignificant as that. You are pretty, intelligent."

From the way he said it, she couldn't tell if he said she was pretty intelligent or pretty and intelligent. She did not believe it. One of them had sucker punched her again. Again she was hard, taken. It didn't matter how he complimented her or didn't compliment her – she didn't like this man.

"If you have no other questions for me…" he said, it didn't seem like that was a question. She had no questions. Still while he was easing out the door she liked she was really going to go off screaming at him "Wait, wait, my mouth is too small. I need collagen to give me that pouty look." Her lips were thin (a little odd for a Black woman but sometimes a gene just skips a generation). Would he have been more receptive if that were her request? Is that safe for Blacks or is there lip skin also very, very particular? Should she cut her losses? See what needs to be nipped or tucked at 24. Maybe this doctor could give her back her C-cups.

Alone in the room she gasped for air. It got to her. This isn't self-improvement damnit. She was not one of those beauty-craving leeches filling his calendar. She was different.

It was bright in the room. It stressed her scar. Light was cruel to her. Highlighting, distressing, disturbing. Devouring.

She just wanted to be happy. Since the loss of her child, this scar was a reminder; she just wanted to be free. These doctors don't care or wonder or understand, they just deliver their next patient.

She'd even gone to a mental doctor. Her and Tracy tried counseling. The doctor said she and her husband were giving "this event" too much power.

"When was the last time you lost a daughter?" Tracy shot back and threw the shrink's coffee mug against the wall.

Jaclyn wouldn't call her husband angry, just expressive. The shrink said that Tracy's revenge on the assailant was wrong-headed because it interfered with their grieving process. He said that Tracy should go for even more anger management classes than what the court had contracted him for. After each anger management class, Tracy would go on for a least an hour about how the facilitator was an underfeed-patch-on-the-elbow-professor- looking-bright-yellow-shiny-happy-button-down-shirt-wearing motherfucker. Jaclyn surmised that anger classes only made Tracy angrier.

Jaclyn grinned and said to her, "Maybe they are all motherfuckers."

The nurse checked back on her and Jaclyn rose to her feet. Just why was she lingering in that room? She hated medical rooms with their clean and white veneer like a piece of driftwood floating. She was sick of this so-called after care. The jungle of room plants and lobby chairs filled with white women and the port-of-wine stains down their throats. Their cleft palates and worse off the worried well whose faces were dropping by time.

There was nothing left to do but go home. Home. A whole year had passed and she and Tracy still hadn't taken down Ella's things. They didn't go in that room, except to put more stuff in. They used it as a storage place like a rental. A dumping ground for junk mail, nick knacks, old sweaters, shoes without heels. Covering maple furniture, the crib, crib canopy, three-drawer base, and four chest. They had really spent a year together. Over $4,000. Quite a bit to a personal banker and music teacher. It's not the money, it's the dream.

Jaclyn's little girl was named after her favorite singer, Ella Fitzgerald — the woman's whose voice could caress you like a mother. When Jaclyn was home alone, she played "How High the Moon" and "Heart and Soul" over and over again.

Tracy put the magazine down when he saw his wife. He stood up. Their eyes connected as he asked her how things went. She blinked and looked away.

When they reached the car, Tracy opened the door as he always did for her but before she could get in he asked,

"Hey, you want to talk about it?"

She shook her head. "No, Trace, I don't."

He spun her around and he bundled her up in his arms, squashing her scant breasts with a clumsy, loving embrace.

"Why are you even at another damned doctor?" he asked. "It's been a year, Jaclyn, you've got to change. Maybe you could get a part time job somewhere. Start putting some effort into your life. I don't want you to go back to teaching though."

Not teach? Her mind rushed ahead with her music degree, there's plenty of will-that-be-paper-or-plastic jobs that she'd be qualified for.

"I wouldn't want you to go back to that. I wouldn't feel safe with you there. I just want you to get out of the house. You can't stay inside all day long only coming out for doctors' appointments—this is nothing to look forward to."

In this open bay, people passed by. She blocked them out. She liked being held and had forgotten how to ask for it. He patted her on the ass then settled her in the car.

"... And for the love of God please throw out all that marigold extract, that Vitamin E, Aloe Vera. All those creams and bottles. Donate them to the local cosmetic bin. Let the homeless people exfoliate."

She looked at him deadpan as he took his place. He stared at the windshield for a few moments. Before starting the car, he signed and said, "Peach, I know it's gotten bad between us. I know you're probably sick of me."

She noticed how far back he was sitting yet how close to the steering wheel he was. Since her attack, she surmised he'd moved up to 250, maybe even 260 pounds. Chalk another one up for GW. She was bothered by his alcohol consumption. After dinner, he now liked that malt liquor with the real high proof.

And he'd asked her if she was sick of him. "I'm not." She answered.

"Yes, you are. I know exactly what you're thinking—he talks about the white man too much."

At that she giggled, drying her eyes with the back of her hand.

He smirked. "I knew that would squeeze a smile out of you."

He was still such an attractive man to her. She liked the way, he preened a little still, knowing he didn't just look good, he looked damn good. He had that ability to make quite the dapper impression, even with the extra weight. He had on an impeccable tailored worsted wool suit coat and slacks. Something about the fabric allowed everything about him to lie flat and smooth and made him look thirty pounds lighter. He would always have his tallness, his intelligence—a little loose with the stars but in an odd way profound. She liked the way he walked in sort of a strut. And he had those full pouty lips she liked so much. She liked it when he kissed her square on the lips hard. Her full soft lips bullying her skimpy ones. With him, she never thought masculinity was anything to fear.

"You feel hungry at all? You want to stop somewhere?"

"I have lamb chops out. Let's just go home."

He nodded and started up the car. He flicked on the radio and out came the dewy sounds of R. Kelly. Before they left the landing, Jaclyn sobbed. "I don't think anyone can help me with this."

Tracy pulled to the side and went into neutral. "Peach, that's not the only doctor. We can go see another one if you want."

"I don't want to."

"Yes, you do."

"I know I do but, I shouldn't – what I mean is I don't want to want to. We've been to enough. I'm just going to have to accept it. I want to get over this. And I don't want this as a reminder. I don't want to be lost." she choked at this part. "I'm afraid to go out in public and --"

"Peach." He said pulling her in again. "No one on this earth is going to stare at you for that. That's the last thing people notice on a pretty thing like you. I can't even see it now."

He ran his lips over the path of the scar and reassured, "If you can't see it, how did you know where it was?" she asked.

"Cuz, I remember the spot."

She blushed, then smiled then blushed again. Tracy has the softest brown eyes, get close and note that they weren't a brown brown they were instead penny-colored. Small and bright like a new penny.

"Tracy, I want to –" she stopped as she thought Ella would have looked like him. She would have had his eyes. His full lips. Ella even would have acted like him. She would be sweet to her and she'd make her laugh and she'd be very proud of herself. Maybe, she'd even be a little chubby like he had become. Jaclyn drew back. She realized she was wrong to keep going to these doctors who are blind.

She was blind to their blindness and in the same it was that moment when she realized she was tied and shackled—tangled. In her mind, the scar evolved into being even more jagged and cracked. Bumpy, pockmarked like a molehill. She was ugly; life was pointless. She was childless and that fragile bond that was forging between her husband and her severed and he went back to being just some foreign being. It wasn't like this last year. She remembers how happy she was last year when she was pregnant. She enjoyed being female, being black, just being. She realized that she was as blind as the blind doctors with the same cane scratching along the pavement and only last year she was full of sight and she could see to see the fullness of their love, Ella. Ella was feeding off her blood as if it were strawberries. Then George Washington interrupted. That man/boy/creature towering over her omnisciently, laughing, cutting, killing.

She conjured up the image of her attacker. Image after image of him like a movie where the last reel winds back upon it. GW tackled her as she was erasing the G clefts of the board during her free period. She didn't even see him coming. He said all this stuff about how it was going to be and how he never had a pregnant woman and he showed his knife to quiet her but that only made her make more noise. Jaclyn kicked and screamed and a custodian heard the ruckus and came in getting him off of her. Unwrapped, she came to not in her makeshift classroom but about glistening plasma bottles and a beeping machine. A blur of figures in white frocks. Doctors and nurses with their resolute smiles, with their well-meaning smiles, with their apologetic smiles. She couldn't get over that cramped and bewildered moment when another doctor told her "I am sorry, Mrs. Upshaw, your baby is gone." That day brought the next 365. They may as well have told her everything back then told her that her child was dead, her face will have to stay scarred, and they may as well add her marriage was probably over.

Now, traveling southbound in the Camry, Jaclyn felt tension rise in her neck. She rolled her shoulders. Then, her own eyes went fuzzy.

She swallowed, blinked. "Tracy, I - I—"

She felt a tattling boiling up in her system, the needles prick her flesh from the insides out. She felt scarring wounds. Lacerating. Richer and richer toward infinity. Choking her veins.

Each moment is loaned, like an accordion folding out, then folding in.

The air was tainted. The sky looked broken; everything was caddywompus. It was bubbling in her glands this sudden intrinsic malignant urge to get out of the car. To run.

They were around Drexel University at rush hour, on the sides of the street, there were Asian grocers, a flower stand run by a one-legged woman, a few peanut stands, and pretzel stands. Ahead at the intersection, she saw a blind man tap crossing the street. She started a scary raw crying fit like she was being split apart. Tracy put his foot on the gas as the car approached the green light. Her eyes were wild and wet then they felt like heavy weights and she opened the passenger side of the door.

"No." he shouted. He made a grab for her but caught only air. "Jaclyn, no."

He pulled on the break and hurried out of the driver's side. The car was rear-ended by a Volvo. Tracy didn't look back.

Jaclyn accelerated her run through the network of cars she moved in this six-lane street as if invincible. She went in front of some cars and behind others. She traveled diagonally. She went in between a Nissan and a Ford. The Ford driver began honking at her just then a Range Rover stepped on its breaks inches before her.

"Crazy bitch." The Nissan driver got out of his car and shook his fist.

When it seemed like she would make it to the pavement, her night dark hair free in the wind as this broke with reality, a Blue Buick Skylark wiggled through at 30 miles per hour, determined to get home in time for evening news.

It was then that she came to her senses, as that machine came right toward her.

At the last possible second, the Skylark swerved and connected with a "No Parking 4pm to 6pm" sign on the pavement instead of her.

A crowd formed to look at the dents and the shards of glass and the crazy lady. Tracy pushed himself to the front of the instant community to claim her. It was similarly to how he found her in the hospital after the attack. Well, but lifeless. The doctors told him she had collapsed after the news of Ella. Here, she again had fainted. Just like women do in those old movies. Life just gets to be too, too much. They fall out from the excitement.

Tracy wrapped his arms around her limp body like gauze.

The Benefit of Doubt

Don't swear, respect your elders, don't hold grudges, love your enemies, always give a fella the benefit of the doubt are the adages that his folks always told him to live by. The first time Dana met his then girlfriend's mom was in 1993. They went over to her North Philly apartment to take her out to lunch. This Miss Hobbes opened the door like she wasn't going to let them in. She stood there up and downing them, just appraising and appraising.

"Well, well, well, if it isn't Miss Hincty Dinkty herself coming to see the everyday people," she told Susan. Then she eyed Dana and said to her, "So you like them light, too."

The smell of alcohol was abundant in her place. Her hair was dyed orange and was so dry looking it seemed ready to be chopped into cornmeal. She was wearing a cheap, stained shirt and her bra straps were showing. The straps were dirty, like she never threw the bra in the wash. Her lumpy shape was spilling out of her dungarees. Even her breath was funky.

The light from the lamp sliced through the blinds and made horizontal lines across the older Miss Hobbes.

In these first few seconds, Dana concluded that she was the ugliest woman he had ever seen.

Dana bit his tongue and looked way. A television in the window across the street was showing a soap opera.

He saw sand run through the hourglass.

"We came to take you out, Momma," Susan said.

Miss Hobbes sucked her teeth, looking at Dana, "Why don't you take your own Momma out?"

"My mother passed away," he told her.

"Did you kill her?" she asked, then dissolved into a cackling laugh.

"Momma, please, we came to take you out—"

Miss Hobbes really started to fuss. "I ain't going anywhere. I got to do my hair." She laughed some more. "I got to rewind the toilet paper roll."

Dana told Susan he'd wait outside. He left her apartment, wiping his shoes on the way out. Outside, he saw two kids, about four or five, playing in the trash chute. They kept sticking their heads in. Dana ran over and told them to stop before they hurt themselves. One of them kicked Dana in the shins and then they both ran away.

Then he heard: "You're nothing special, Susan. He's not going to stay with you. He's just using you till he finds something better."

Tracy went back toward the door.

"What kind of name is Dana? Is he a faggot? Dana's a faggot's name. Susan, is your boyfriend a faggot?"

Susan came out of her mother's apartment visibly shaken. "She's drunk."

"No kidding," Dana said.

"I was hoping we'd catch her right. When she's not so bad. This time of the day. She'll like getting out. We can order one of one of those drinks where you keep the glass."

"You know you don't have to take that off her," Dana said.

"She's all I have left," Susan said. She never knew her father. Her grandmother passed ten years ago. Her older brother was doing seven to fifteen for involuntary manslaughter.

Just then, her mother came out into the hall. "Y'all niggers still here?"

"Momma—" Susan began.

"We were just leaving." Dana told her, taking Susan's hand and inching her away.

They ended up going to Red Lobster. The one in Clifton Heights that had turned into a black family reunion. They ordered all you can eat shrimp (fried, grilled, scampied) and had greasy, cheddar butter bread. Red Lobster was owned by the Quaker Oats Company. Dana knew that; he was a business major.

In booth six, Dana and Susan spoke to one another. Dana went over to her side of the table and held her. He remembered something his folks always told him: Some days will be worse than others.

When Susan and Dana married two years later, Miss Hobbes didn't show up for the wedding.

The deejay played "Ribbon in the Sky" by Stevie Wonder and outside on that hazy, early June day, the sun was beating down. Everyone who came was well behaved and wished them well. The young couple settled into a steady flow of life.

When he received the phone call, Dana had almost everything in life—a loving wife, beautiful daughter, a nice career, a good home. "Mr. Lewis, this is Mercy Fitzgerald. Your mother-in-law has been hospitalized."

His eyes scrunched closed as he thought to himself could this really be the end. False alarms had gone off before. He savored the moment with one single clap of his hands and told his secretary that he'd be gone for the rest of the day.

He usually was solemn when visiting the hospital, but on that day there was a bounce in his step. He joyously walked through the corridors and watched people wheeling gurneys with a smile on his face.

After being briefed formally on the graveness of his mother-in-law's condition, he went straight for her room.

Her face was like a mask, a frozen expression of anguish like a black harlequin. Her eyes were red except for the black dots in the center. Her body was about the same—lumpy and thick under freshly laundered white sheets.

"They tell me this is it," he said, "So I'm going to give this to you quick. I've been watching you, year in and year out, put my wife through hell. Every time you needed money. Every time you needed to be picked up because you were stranded somewhere. Every time you needed to be bailed out. In the meantime, we have had a daughter. She's four. You didn't send a freaking card or a fucking balloon. But I knew. I knew this day would finally come. I knew your ways would catch up with you. We would finally be rid of you. I mean this from the bottom of my heart: I am truly overjoyed. It is so good to see you."

There, he had said his peace. Now it was time to turn and leave.

"Hey, you."

Dana turned.

"You can't let me out of the world like that."

"Didn't you just hear me? I don't give a shit how you go out of the world."

"Where is my daughter?"

"Susan is on her way. She's coming from upstate. Our daughter—"

"I don't want to hear all that shit. I asked you when she will be here," she hissed.

"What do you care about? Unloading at this late hour, trying to make yourself free."

"I'll say what I want. She was my daughter before she was your wife. Don't you ever forget that! I run this show."

"Like hell, you do, you ugly bitch."

She laughed. "All these years. All these fucking years, I thought you were the strong, silent type. Now, I see you're just like any other nigger."

"You're calling me a nigger?"

"Yes, nigger," she yelled and kept raging, "And you better be glad I'm not well. If I was I would get up and break my foot off in your ass, you fucker. You goddamn phony, you think you're so much better than me. You and Susan are perfect for each other. I wouldn't give you two niggers five dollars a year," she continued. She enjoyed the reaction she got and went for more.

"Come on. You want to hit me don't you? Do it. Do it already."

It took all the strength he had to not follow her command.

"You better not do it, you chicken shit. I'm a sick woman. I'm touch and go."

"Go," he said and slammed the door behind him.

Out in the quiet, ivory hallway, he felt a weightless, cool breeze. His smile had faded. She was having the last laugh after all. He could hear her voice is in his head. Her cackling laugh.

"Daddy!" His daughter came running down the hall well ahead of her mother. She looked very much the miniature, mirror image. Same wide set eyes. Same undersized top lip, same undersized lower lip.

"Dana," Susan said. These days, she wore her hair chin length with a side part. It covered her left eye. Her face was brown and stained from tears.

Dana stretched his arms open for both his girls. He held them tight for a good long while and told them nothing of the exchange he'd just had.

Next, they went back into the room.

Dana stood back against the wall and folded his arms. He still wanted to put his hands around her throat and strangle her.

He observed his wife and child, thinking he must be missing something. Missing something huge. He scratched his head, perplexed. It was like there was no bad history between them.

Susan and Lisa were by her bedside. They offered her comforting, consoling hands.

Miss Hobbes took one look at the two of them, breathed in their compassion, and expired.

Kris

The phone rings and you avoid answering it. It's late. Ten post meridian is late for you. You've already been to bed and in your pajama bottoms. By the sixth ring, the party gives up. Over, so you think but within seconds it rings again. You opt to pick it up this time, sourly thinking this better be good.

"Hello, Kris?"

All of a sudden your heart stops then you smile. You know the voice. An image swirls through your mind and you listen to Ann's voice. She tells you she's just blowing back into town after a long interstate drive. She said she'd just taken a trip down South. She said she wanted to be back where it was warm. Back where she could get back her accent. It didn't matter about the rednecks; she just wanted to be home for a while.

She tells you she never tossed your number. She said she's dying to see you she's sorry she woke you.

"Where are you?" you ask.

"At a diner." she said it with a fetching sort of magnolia drawl.

"Why don't you come here?"

"...It's better that you come here. I mean I want to talk to you about us. I don't want to start anything, right away. I just want to see you."

You ask her where the diner is that she's at. "I'm at the Flameburger. I won't keep you up late."

"You know me. I already think it's late."

"Well then I won't keep you up too much later." You promise you will be there in fifteen minutes it's ten minutes away. You throw on a T-shirt and some clunky shoes, and you wrap yourself up in a bulky black overcoat.

Outside the icy wind whips back your hair around so angrily as you make your way down the road but all of a sudden you stopped short. You stand still.

You just can't do it.

You just can't make yourself go there and say, "Really, really…" and you smile. You can't make yourself go there and say really really and smile as she lifts the coffee cup to your lips and she talks about the sweetness of Raleigh. You can't smile and you can't order a hamburger and laugh and pick up the check cuz she says, "No, no, I'll cover it" and you say, "Well, Okay" as you smile and spring for the tip.

You remember the last time you saw her she was with another girl buying cards at the only openly gay women's bookstore in town. When you saw her with the girl your smile stopped the emptiness that filled up inside you it's only a matter of time the lesbian population in Madison is so incestuous, relationships and marriage and contort. You'd see the two over and over again, not only at your bookstore, but at your dance club and your part of the park.

No one belongs to anyone and now she wants to talk and have coffee at the Flameburger.

You can't do it, not again.

You start walking back to your apartment. Because you are now walking against it, the wind is kind. You wonder if Eliana would have employed the old standbys, "... I knew it wouldn't last between her and me... I didn't love her ... I only love..."

For you, that would be so nice to hear in a born-again Southern accent, even nicer to believe as you reenter your sparse apartment, alone.

Troubadour

Every inch of the park was filled with Katrina's family and more reunionees were coming in, wedging their way through the crowd. They were sitting on folding chairs, kitchen chairs, dining room chairs, stools, and plastic covered sofa. Devron, Katrina's boyfriend, felt he was going to heaven. Devron hadn't been surrounded by this many blacks since grade school. A private school scholarship for music made him used to whites. He liked their parties where he could be the black olive sinking to the bottom of the clear martini. He was so used to their rules: carriage, dress code, comportment and exhibiting lady/gentlemen like behavior. Now, this scene made him recall some backwater town down South or some dead-end street in Harlem with all this soul music, deep-fried chicken, and lemonade. Katrina's mother kept circulating with a plate of this or a pitcher of that and her face had that country freshness, that shine. Katrina's brother Fred was loud, telling recycled Def Jam riffs. His gold tooth showed yet he wasn't the only one who had this fashion statement, there was also Katrina's West Indian bangled Aunt Toni, she reminded Devron of that fat woman from the 14 bus with Acme bags.

Sensing his discomfort but blind to its source, Katrina kept starting conversations with Devron about politics or religion or talk shows or sports but these people kept coming up to them and interrupting with the same question: "You're an opera singer? I thought they were all fat and white."

Devron offered a frozen smile. Dervon was thin and black. Tenors, usually, didn't look like him yet he had played all the best roles, Samson and, of course, Othello. His voice had crystalline beauty and range of colors. The Black voice is an instrument dark and heavy.

"Sing!" was always the follow up request.

Katrina nudged him, saying, "Now, you know why I don't carry my cello around everywhere I go."

Devron could sing in German and Italian but he shook his head. He wasn't going to vocalize for them not when his mind kept racing with images like drivebys and drug use. Dope addicts and 'hos. The atmosphere was too much for him.

Though Katrina looked like she was on close terms with the treadmills, her mother looked like Florida on *Good Times*. Her little sister was a horror too. She was too skinny, knock-kneed. What kind of sense did it make. Katrina was almost 30 and her sister was only 12. Dervon noticed black families were always like this, a random assortment. Absolute chaos. Devron believed that White families had children in perfect space three years apart.

Her relatives were still coming, closing in on him.

This wasn't him, he wanted to take him out of his past situation, a voice like a star. Stars belong in the sky. Devron excused himself by saying to Katrina that he had to use the restroom, and he rationalized it as he walked away. He was used to the very expensive, elitist operatic world. (A good deal of unnecessary typecasting as far as ethnic or "racial" back-ground goes.) There, directors and designers and producers told him directly "I will not hire a black for this role" or "I can't sell a black tenor." Devron appreciated the honesty. What's the difference between saying someone is too heavy or too short and saying someone is too black? This wasn't a foible that you can't easily do something about like close-set eyes.

Devron treated quickly through the crowd.

"Where are you going, Honey?" asked that walking lava lamp, Katrina's Aunt Melvina. She had on this horrid yellow dress and on her head was this wig she got out of the back of a wig catalogue. Devron felt so lightheaded.

"Away," Devron told her and continued to make his break for it.

Driving away felt so, so good. Driving, being in the open air everything felt better. His neck joints felt loose. Senior fluids flowed freely. There was no reason to feel bad about it; this is what he wanted. It was his life. He had a right to live it the way he wanted. He didn't have to explain anything.

When he got home, he had five messages on the answering machine, each message was a little more frantic. He waited an obligatory two hours to call her back.

"I just wasn't feeling well," he told Katrina.

"Well, why didn't you say that?"

"I did."

"No, you didn't. You said you had to go to the bathroom."

"That's what I meant."

"Since when do you confuse a toilet seat with your car seat."

Devron pictured her slim neck rolling, her brown eyes bulging – the way black women get at times like this.

"Katrina, I have to go," he said quickly.

"Where?" she asked.

Devron hung up. Early the next morning, she came to his apartment in jeans and a tee shirt. On her head, she wore a Black Kangol hat that flopped. That's another thing he hated about black women; they didn't show their hair everyday. They wigged it when they couldn't dig it, or they wore hats. Devron believed that white women never had to worry about that.

"What's wrong?" Katrina asked.

"Nothing's wrong."

"I thought you said you weren't feeling well."

"That was yesterday. I'm getting kind of busy."

"You're busy," she paraphrased.

Silence.

"If you're busy, I'll catch you some other time," Katrina said and turned to leave. She slammed the door behind her.

Later she called him saying, "We never really had an intense relationship but I thought this was leading somewhere."

"We were leading somewhere but --."

"But? But? But what? What?" she asked.

"Maybe we need a little time apart," he said but he really wanted to tell her the truth. He felt he owed her at least that.

Katrina was baffled. Absolutely baffled yet, if she would have thought in the right direction it would have come to her. Back in college, she had gone on a blind date. She answered a personal ad that didn't specify race. That night she met up with a medium heighted, slight build man with yellow blond hair. He was sitting in the waiting area with a full bouquet of roses by his side. As she approached him, she brightened. As he saw her, he dimmed.

"You are Katrina?" he asked.

"Yes, you're David."

His eyebrows raised then lowered. "You didn't tell me you were black."

"You didn't ask."

"You said you were a cellist."

"I am."

"You're a cellist?" he asked.

"I'm a black cellist," she answered.

"This is not going to work."

"What's not going to work? It's just dinner."

"Dinner's not going to work. I didn't know you were black. You don't even sound black."

Katrina blinked. "I flunked Ebonics in high school."

"Right there." He shocked his middle finger. "You don't sound black at all."

The hostess came by with her brown hair split down the middle and even features and a fixed smile. "A table is available now. Please follow me."

"Could you just give us a few minutes?" David told the hostess. He waited till she left then he looked dead into Katrina's deep eyes. "I wanted a romantic relationship. Here." He tried to hand her the roses, she wouldn't take them. He then got up and walked away.

Katrina's gaze traveled, following him. He went straight to his car and ignited its engine. He'd left the white roses on the bench beside her.

"Is there something wrong?" the hostess came back and asked.

Numb. Stunned. Katrina rose to her feet and ambled to the door vowing never to place another ad.

The hostess called after her. "Wait, you forgot your flowers."

During the dry spells in her love life (and there were many), Katrina thought of that misbegotten night. She had gone to that restaurant with such hope. They had such great conversations over the phone...

She had gone out with Devron for almost a year. The hard part was explaining his absence to her mom and her Aunt Melvina. They were so happy that she was dating a nice young man, an opera singer.

Devron always swallowed a tablespoon of olive oil before each performance. Katrina found him in the warm up room past the racks and racks of old costumes.

"Devron, how many tenors does it take to change a light bulb?" she asked him.

"I don't know."

"One."

"I don't get it, Katrina."

"One holds it in place and the world revolves around him."

The next six years took them to different places. Not so much geographically but metaphysically. Katrina abandoned music and moved out of the downtown. She picked up a job as a receptionist at a law firm. They kept her at ¾ time so they could avoid granting health insurance. However, there was one perk to the job; she began dating an attorney. She was surprised when it started to get steady. Within eight months and practicing to say 36, she got married and worked only half time. Feng shui. That was what her new life was like. Even deeper into the burbs. No clutter. No baggage. Not even her cello and bow was over her. So open and airy. She was expecting her first child.

In contrast, music was all Devron Evans had. His operatic career took off like a guided missile. Though critical acclaim was elusive, he had a successful pop opera thing happening thanks to national exposure of singing "America the Beautiful" at a World Series game. Critics found his voice "earthy". He was featured in *Ebony* and *Time*. All the articles gushed, bespeaking his instruments unspeakable gorgeousness. Next came The Met, then *Larry King Live*. Training up to seven hours a day, he heard the success he always, always dreamed of, but he was still solo. Though he was on a steady diet of women of the caucasian persuasion, he was still searching. From time to time, he netted the occasional Midwestern blonde. Most of the time, he defaulted to New York brunettes. Often they were older than him and when they leaned forward an inch of gray hair would show at the root. These were liberal's daughters who always seemed to want him to regal them with tragedy. The plight of the black man tales. One woman he was seeing used to bring him clippings from grassroot rags on the "struggle". Stuff about the third world and freeing Mumia. Devron didn't get it. In the media, he'd seen a lot of examples of successful black men who linked white women. Were all those brothers putting up with this? Maybe, he was too sensitive. Too analytical. He thought too deeply about things.

The key to happiness is to stay superficial. Devron was convinced of that.

On one of her rare trips downtown, Katrina happened by a bus shelter. What was advertised took her breath away. Katrina walked inside it and stared at the enlargement of Devron's ebony face. A deluge of emotions hit her even though it had been years. That night, she went online and bought two tickets. She had two dressy pregnancy dresses. One in black that was lacy and lavender satin one. She chose the one in purple which played nicely against her brown skin.

That night, her husband called to tell her he was running a little late, so they wouldn't have time to catch dinner before. What with the expressway and parking and time ticking, ticking, the show was well underway by the time they arrived. Devron was in a deep emotional rendition of "Nessun Dorma."

(If you are close enough to the stage that you can see their eyes they can see yours.) Katrina could swear the tuxedo Devron noticed them hustling down the center isle.

Devron's eyes jetted from his ex-girlfriend with her husband. He lingered on her accompaniment. Her husband was a cross between Superman and Gaston from *Beauty and the Beast*. That lantern jawed, that dark brown hair, those hazel eyes.

As a credit to Devron's dedication, his troubadour presence, he never missed his cue as his mind galloped.

Devon's eyes couldn't get past the contrast of Katrina's husband's white skin against Katrina's nonwhite skin. Devron sang about a mythical battle, as his eyes moved back and forth between Katrina and her mate. He held his heart as it sank, he vocalized the last line "Je Vaincre". English translation, "I shall win."

The Process

The horses whined, the mules brayed, and people got sold. Me included. That's what I was there for: a price.

I could hear myself breathing as the air stilled around me. Fear set in.

The sun's heat wasn't that strong, but I was swimming in sweat.

For a second, I almost prayed. Just like all the other times I'd been up for sale, I'd hoped that I wouldn't be herded out. I wished that somehow they'd let me be for once. Leave me alone. Let me stand on that block for to find my own eternity. But, this was about money and tradition and the law. I knew this part so well. The selling process was the thing that was followed by the mystery. I'd be forced into a question, a new place, like a drop of rain falling from the sky; I had no say in where I'd fall.

"He looks well fed enough, but is he obedient?" one bidder asked.

"He is. You can bet good money on it," the slave seller promised, his voice bleeding with a different kind of fear.

I was the last one left, everyone else had a bill of sale.

I wasn't in a collar or manacled to the post: I had the kind of chains that don't give, ever. The kind that weren't visible. I stood there all the same. It was all the same as all them finely dressed folk eyed me like a prize mare, testing me, feeling the muscles in my arms.

In a parade, person after person spied me, appraised me, and judged me. Some seemed grasping as if looking without knowing what they were looking for. They looked up my nostrils and into the whites of my eyes.

I refused to blink.

As potential buyers noted the condition of my teeth, I caught sight of their appearance? All their given warts and pock marks.

"This one here ain't no lazybones," the slave seller boasted of me trying to win back their attention even as they strolled away in clusters.

They didn't believe him.

My whip marks to them proved otherwise. Everyone knew lazybones get the whip. And my scars were deep, deep as marks in Jesus' palm. People thought the worst. In their mind, they sketched scenarios of wild rebellion.

"We treat slaves like they're family," a woman with the parasol said, "We usually don't have to get physical."

"Then this one would be a good fit. Seeing that he's already broken in," the slave seller said, changing his sales pitch.

The slave seller's well-placed words were a little too late. Before long, the next round of onlookers approached and he snapped back into form.

"Step right up. Get in as close as you like," the seller said.

The woman, who was surrounded by other ladies and gentleman in well-designed garments, just nodded and walked away. I was familiar with her type—I watched and considered. People like her might have kindness in their voice at first, but they were no better than the rest. They were still looking for constant labor and if ever you didn't deliver they know how to make hell.

The seller continued to speak highly of me.

But that group moved on.

Another fill of people came by, and I began to consider which one would pay for me? Which would take me as property to their property and would that place be like big with lots of silverware and candlesticks and rows and rows of cotton to pick or would it be a far less grand spot, with only a narrow lot to till over.

Maybe no one would buy me, I thought again. I hoped again. Then stopped myself. I would stay the day until I was sold and then come back the next day and the next day after that until I was moved.

The heat settled on me and was here to stay.

There was not, nor would there ever be for me more to life than growing rice and picking cotton. There was no need kidding myself, trying to keep that little something I used to have in reserve. That part that wanted adventure and fun. That part that thirsted to be free. I might as well lose that portion too.

"Twelve, huh?" someone asked.

The slave seller, perked up, nodded agreeing to the lie.

I wasn't. I was ten and five, but they listed me as ten and two to get more money. Certain things sell better so often life stories change. Years get subtracted or added. Even blood gets altered. If they can, they'll pass you off as mixed, or even quadroon or octoroon. If they can convince people that you are not pure, but part of the buffer race, that way you seem more refined, cultivated and civilized. But anyone could plainly see that I didn't have skin yellow as ripe corn or my black hair didn't grow in ringlets. Nevertheless, my face was smooth of stubble and light brown – so it was on the same round as believable that I was mulatto lad who had yet to shave. The truth was I didn't know what to believe about my age or most anything else—I knew little of my mother and nothing of my father.

As soon as I learned to walk, my mother was sold one direction and I was sold another. I was raised, (when I was raised) by someone else's mom.

As far as father ... fathers weren't important, I was told.

"Got some marks on him," that same man commented then eased along.

A scrap of my thoughts lifted as I saw beyond the block to the trees and sky all around. I love to look out and see things. The air stirred right then, but went back to not circulating.

I'd been sold five times before. Once because of gambling debts, another time because of divorce, twice due to death. This time I was sold on the count of my master's moving. He'd had enough of his plantation on the Mississippi river and was going back to green grass of Edinburgh, Scotland.

It's nice to have a choice in where you go and what you do.

As the last drop of daylight left, the slave seller got desperate. He looked at me like a cat looked at a cornered mouse.

He went to pull people in with promises, "Strong and healthy and can work all day."

"Fine looking boy," a man in an ascot said nodding. "What does he answer?"

"Whatever you want him to," the seller said.

The accosted man moved closer, and my heart sank further.

He, too, wanted to see if my mouth is filled with teeth.

"Open," the slave seller said.

I did, but I didn't speak.

Silence was my friend.

I did listen.

"You'll get a lot of hard work out of him."

After this inspection, there was private talk between seller and potential buyer and then the magic words were spoken:

"Sold!"

Mother Love

Her voice came across to me: smooth and deep, bedroom-ish, almost, but I could tell she had it on a leash. She had it controlled on the edge of passion, it was a game she loved to play with men, like tap dancing on a trap door.

"Breakfast is ready," she called to me from the foot of the stairs.

I was sitting in my playroom, in a bean bag chair, legs crossed and my shoe laces untied, ready to implode from the anticipation.

"I'll be right down, Ma," I replied.

I don't know what part of my anatomy yearned to be satiated the most – my stomach? My heart? My… eyes?

I flew downstairs, with wings.

"Mother!" I exclaimed, with my arms flung open.

"You're not dressed for school," she observed, patting me on my noggin, like the sexual beast that she was.

"I don't feel well," I lied. There was nothing wrong with me, I was the proverbial picture postcard of health, I just wanted her to lapse into that "Oh, where does it hurt" routine.

"Well, it kinda hurts all over." I told her, ambiguously.

Then she felt me, up and down, quizzing me as she poked my ribs and squeezed my thighs. "Here? Here? Where does it hurt? Point it out?"

I couldn't tell her, I was speechlessly lost in the euphoria of her probing. After a while, however, she gave up.

"Drink some milk," she advised. To Ma, milk was the panacea. She swore to me that, that fortified liquid whiteness would bleach away all my pains... Ma acted naïve like that sometimes.

I asked her to pause with me, to hold my hand till the anguish localized, for my aches to find haven elsewhere. She told me she had things to do, floors to scrub, windows to wipe and that if I stayed home, I'd just be in the way so I should down my milk like a good little boy and stand at the bus corner like a nice little student.

"I don't like school," I said.

"It's good for you," Mother told me.

"You're good for me."

"You're not old enough to know what's good for you."

"I'm old enough to know − " I told her, pausing for dramatic effect. "—that I want to marry you."

"I'm already married."

"Can't you get a divorce?"

"You are being ridiculous."

"I am ridiculous, ridiculously in love with you, Babe!" I confessed. "And you said you love me, Ma." I continued morning my evidence. "You tell me you love me every night and plant a big wet kiss on my forehead."

"I do the same thing to your sister."

"But that's different, my sister's a girl. You can't marry a girl."

"I can't marry a boy either."

"You married Daddy and he's a boy."

"He's a man," she corrected.

"I'll be a man … someday," I said prophetically.

"You're not talking sense. Go to school," she ordered.

"Okay, I'll go," I said. "But if I learn something, it won't be because I want to."

And I marched upstairs to change from my night clothes into my day clothes, thinking Moms are such a tease.

Deconstruction

In the name of the Father, the Son, and the ... oh, you know the rest... I'm Sister Ardeth Margaret Katherine D'Arby, and I have just been sentenced to three years. He knows what He's doing. It will be three years well spent, that I assure you. Those souls locked away need my guidance, and it won't be my first time on the inside, as they say. It won't be so bad. I hope we will be able to stay together though — myself with the other Sisters Jacqueline and Carol. I pray that they won't split us up. I've known them since I first entered the order. We were so young then, thinking we could save the world...

The judge had such harsh words for us. Such harsh words. He said we were "dangerously irresponsible." To that Sister Carol said, "Nuclear warfare is dangerously irresponsible!" And that judge told her to Shut Up! Shut up, he said. Imagine such talk. Shut up, he said.

Some government property should be destroyed. All the papers made such a big deal about the blood. We used our blood to make crosses on the missiles. I've been with the order for 20 years. I would do it again.

And then we used a hammer. Pounding and pounding. If only we could turn it into salt.

Rain

My father was always angry with me angry—violent. He used to shove my face in the dirt out back of our house. His large hands on the back of my neck. I remember that. And I did struggle, while he gritted my nose into the rough rocks, the multicolored pebbles, the slugs, the dogshit.

I still have scars. I have three other brothers, but I was always the one who got it the worst. I got call the worst names and got held under the water the longest. I was the oldest in my family, I guess he wanted me to be a man.

I am a man... more or less.

We all got beat, including Ma until I was 14. I was lucky to get big so early I had farm muscles. My father went to swing at me one Sunday and I like and went crazy on you. He's like a visitation. I kicked my father's miserable ass like I was some kind of psycho. When it was all through my father was bruised up, bleeding on the floor. Blood just milking out of him...

He knew better than to mess with me again and I told him never to scrap the rest of the family, ever.

Well, it was about then that he started drinking, deteriorating. Roaming about the house, pissing on himself with his mouth poked out cuz he'd been dethroned. I didn't feel bad about beating him, shit happens. I dropped out of school the following year, lied about my age to get a garage job and move on my own.

I don't really think about the past anymore. The past has passed, that's what I say. But the reason for all of this reckoning is that it's my turn.

It's my turn to watch my father.

See, my brother, Tony had him for the last eight months, and Ron can't have him because he's in jail on drug-related charges and Bill can't do it because he's over in Korea in the full-time Army and Ma died last year.

So Dad is alone.

So I'm left.

I'm close. I live a whole six miles away from where I grew up. I don't want him, though.

I can't tell you that my wife because I can't tell that to my wife because she's the girl from good beginnings. She had a finishing school accent and together parents, she'd never understand how I grew up, how the other half lives.

My wife's name is Denise. She's a nursery school teacher. She's pretty but just to me. She's too plain and wholesome to be a real turn on. She always wears knee-length A-line skirts. On a brief snit of trying to better myself, I'd meet her at a GED program. She was my tutor. She's always been kind to me and never called me stupid.

When Denise first met my father, she commented "Oh, what a cute little man."

Granted, he had shrunk.

And our little 5-year-old Caralyn, she took a likening to my father. Letting my father pinch her on the cheek and pat her head without her screaming. Caralyn usually ran from strangers. This was very strange.

As for my reaction, I showed my father to the smallest room in the house and told him to only come out for food and water.

He didn't have the balls to defy me so I was fortunate enough not to have to endure his ruddy mug all through supper. Still, I grew sullen just knowing that he was in the same house, fixing himself a little snack plate from my fridge. Using my toilet sleeping in the bed and bedding I provided. What did he think this is some fucking fairytale?

I stopped messing around with my wife.

I started waking up at four in the morning, tapped out only to spend the remainder of the day yawning.

Nothing meant shit to me.

My father had been in country for a month; an enemy with the same facial features and the same last name as myself.

Michelle hounded me, tenderly, rustling her long dark lashes against my cheek. "Johnny, what's the matter, Johnny?"

There was a voice trapped inside my throat. I never answered.

One evening, I knocked off work early. It was about 6:30 p.m. when I came in. Caralyn was sitting on my father's lap, resting her head on his once solid chest. She was showing him pictures she had drawn in her coloring book and Caralyn had small eyeballs and whenever she was amused, her eyes would disappear in the fold and she was laughing and our eyes had disappeared and I was like now wait one Goddamn minute.

Did I tell you to stay in your room ice cream that my father daddy you didn't tell me that Caralyn spoke up mistakenly thinking that I was angry with her.

Michelle came from the kitchen looking bewildered.

You better step off Grandpa I told him then never the coloring book from their hands and threw it against the wall.

"I knew I should have left you fucking and out in the cold," I told him.

"Johnny," Michelle cried "What's come over you?"

"Shut up, woman," I told her. I went up closer to my father. "All you need is a fucking rocking chair and a porch and some freakin' frakin' Country Time lemonade and you'd be grandfather of the year." I yelled and yanked Caralyn office lap and through or on the floor.

Caralyn began to cry so I bare knuckle hit her across the mouth.

"Johnny, why are you acting like this?" Michelle ran over to Caralyn.

"You lousy son-of-a-bitch, I want you out of this house," I said to my father.

Caralyn started crying louder so I hit her again. I grabbed her up by the collar answers shaking her like crazy saying, "You want to live with him or you want to live with me. You want to live with him you want to live with him. Hell, you don't even know him. He's the mean one. How could you go on trusting him? How could you go on believing him? He's nothing to you."

Michelle was struggling with me pleading with me to please, please leave Caralyn now alone.

I wasn't listening. I didn't stop beating my child till I got tired and by that time dang it was bruised black and blue.

My father rose his feet. He began to speak. His voice sounded almost soothing and warm though worn as a well-trampled carpet. All those booze full years it really gravels his voice. "You act like it was all yesterday. It wasn't."

"Get out of my Goddamned house."

"I left you standing I left you with something boy you don't want me to have nothing."

"Get the Hell out of my house."

"Your blood is my blood. Everything you have comes from me." He walked over to the staircase and began the path to his room. He stopped on the fourth step and repeated "I left you standing." He shook his head and walked on.

Michelle took Caralyn to the bathroom to get her wounds cleaned up and I heard my father moving around in the room I had set up for him. It sounded as if he was packing.

As I sat alone in the room hearing voices of my daughters and wife's cries, not wanting to console or help: I thought, why should I feel sorry for them? I don't even feel sorry for myself. I saw it but could give no larger emotion. It was the first time I had hit my daughter or my wife. It was just the worst. So far.

I sighed and sighed again. I sighed the night away and popped open some liquor cans and smoked Marlboros, two at a time. All I did is wonder, does it fall from the sky like rain, this anger?

It's a Sin to Tell a Lie

Mornings always came too early in the day for Paulie, but these things have to be overcome when you reach a certain age the alarm clock sings like zero hour at Chernobyl. Paulie hated the jump through a hoop, Pavlovian salivating a dish mentality of reacting to the sound of a bell. He buried his head in the pillow, deep in a denial state deep in the denial syndrome trying to catch a few more remnants of sleep.

"Honey, wake up. You'll be late for work," his wife Linda whispered in his ear, like reality stepping through a glass window. Then she touched his face with her mouth in a manner that wasn't completely to his pleasure. Though they had been married for two years she had rub down the just hitched Goose pimples she's still impassioned and touching feely, she used every opportunity to spill on him like paint with her body heat or body weight or her moist oral contact probably found it smothering and develop and almost asthmatic reaction to her excess affection as a result.

"All right all right already I'm up for Christ's sake," he helped her as he wiped the liquid of her kiss from his skin.

"I didn't want you to have to rush," she asked quietly smiling apologetically.

"Me? Rush?"

"Well, you know what I mean—I'm sorry, Paulie," she said then began twirling her hair around her fingers, a nervous tick she'd had since he'd known her. "I'll fix you some breakfast … I could fix you some waffles."

"I hate waffles," Paulie said.

"You loved waffles Paulie you have always loved waffles Paulie—always like ever since I've known you."

"Times change."

"Oh, yeah, I guess they do… Do you still like eggs?" Linda asked cautiously.

"If that's all you got I'll take it."

"Good," she said and cheerfully skipped away.

Paulie lay in bed with his eyes closed for a little while longer, wallowing in the void of total darkness. All the while morning seeped through the curtain fringe, like a probation officer calling him back to the chain gang after an all too short night of parole.

Paulie, however, tried to be an adult about it, grabbing grubbing down his scrambled eggs and home fries, then gulping down a glass of orange juice like a good soldier. And he stared at Linda's body in her burgundy Argyle acrylic robe as if it's still excited. It seemed it was seemingly obvious, even if he stretched his imagination to elastic proportions and back again, that thrill was gone.

Linda had accumulated a few inches since he married her yet that was no matter to him. She was never real slender, and besides, it was the littlest thing about her that was the sexiest. Paulie would envision himself nibbling at her ankle or narrowing at the pinkness of her lower lip as he did years prior but now the thought of only sticking to him. He wanted no parts of her—no part at all.

So, when he heard the croaking voice asking "How's your meal?" he answered with a flat, "Just dandy"

Just because there was a noise, a distance a cry of distress louder than the danger alert at Chernobyl, even louder than his Emerson alarm clock.

The baby's crying, she said with apprehension I hope there's nothing wrong with him.

"Why don't you go find out?" he suggested more out of desire to get her out of sight then any concern for the baby

"All right, Paulie," she agreed, wiping her hands on her apron giving him a sloppy kiss on the size of his face before she toddered away.

Paulie felt like getting drunk, blowing off work and getting down to Corky's Steak and Ale and finishing off a bottle of cheap vodka, as if it was lemonade. But he thought "nah" cuz that's how he spent the previous day.

"Why me" he wondered *"what have I done to deserve this?"*

"Marriage will be good for you," Paulie's mother promised him. "It will give it some responsibility."

"Yeah, breaking my back for chump change working like a horse till I start thinking like a horse trying to support that broad living the rest of my life without a pot to piss in or a window to throw it out of all because of her. I wanted to get out of this piss hole of a town. I wanted to see the world."

"Stop that filthy talk before I slap your face!" his mother snapped. "You know you don't want that baby to grow up without a father. You know how you feel about your daddy deserting you and your brothers. You don't want some poor child to feel the same way about you. That would be shameful. That would be a sin to God."

"God? God? God? don't talk to me about God I'm talk to you about me."

"And I'm talking to you about something bigger than you or me. Be reasonable, as an adult you made a mistake now owned up to it."

"Do I have to spend the rest of my life owning up to it while I don't love her?"

"That's a horrible thing to say."

"It's the truth... I don't care about her—it was just one of those late-night things I never loved her. It wasn't planned. I didn't mean to do I have to spend the rest of my life with her and that brat cursing the day I ever laid eyes on her?"

"You did a lot more than just lay eyes on her."

"She let me."

"You wanted to that night or those nights or whatever. You got what you wanted."

"That's only one way to look at it, Ma, but that still doesn't erase the fact that I don't want her—now."

"It's not important what you want anymore. Linda is a sweet girl, a nice girl. How can you stand to break her heart?"

"How can you take her side in this?"

"I'm not taking her side in this I'm taking that three-month-old fetus' side."

"That thing's not even real yet. It's not even really alive yet."

"I don't want to continue this discussion anymore."

"So, I knocked her up. I'm sorry, Ma. I'll apologize till the day I die. I'm sorry about it now."

"Paulie, you're a father. There's nothing else you can do about it, everything except the right thing."

"And what is that, Ma."

"Marry her."

"Marry her? I don't even love her. I don't even like her. You want me to marry a woman I can't stand?"

"You won't be the first guy who did."

"The hell…" he began.

"End it, Paulie. No more talk."

"The hell I will, Ma…." he began again.

"End it I said," then she smacked him. She smacked him square across his seventeen-year-old face with the resentment that she harbored in her thirty-one-year-old unwed mind. "Now, you do the right thing, and you marry that girl."

Meanwhile, Linda was giggling the baby on her lap and offering Paulie a penny for his thoughts.

"Nothing I was thinking anything."

"You've been falling into trances a lot lately, Paulie. You must be thinking about something," she said sweetly Linda was sweet if nothing else she was as sweet as a restful dream.

"No, nothing," he lied "Nothing at all… I better get ready for work." She and the baby had been leaning too closely on him; it felt it made him feel itchy and antsy. He had to stand up quickly and get somewhere even if it was to that ten-hour-a-day slave pit.

"Wait," Linda implored him, grabbing the cuff of his shirt with a tug hoping to grass his finger or hold his hand but he was moving too quickly away from her.

"What do you want for me now?"

She didn't notice the hardness of his tone—she never did.

"You'll be away from me for a whole ten hours, Paulie. I don't know how I'll manage," she said.

"Try hard."

"Wait, Paulie, please?" she asked him, setting the baby down on the crib.

Paulie obliged and waited by the door.

Linda came running up and gave him a long kiss. Then she opened her eyes and told him sincerely, "Oh, Paulie, I love you so."

"Yeah... likewise," he replied.

Killing in Periot

I wasn't just Solly's brother; I was his protector. Over the years, I had done a pretty good job of it considering what I was up against. Nick was my stepfather. He was Solly's real father. He was our main adversary. Everyone else, I could handle.

It all came to a crossroad late that fall when I was fifteen, nearly sixteen, and Solly was younger than that. We both upped our ages so we could work long hours at shit jobs because that was what Nick told us to do. Nick pimped us out to honest jobs since his own illegal exploits were going slow. Between Solly and me, we pulled an all-right grip; the only hitch was Nick took it all.

Now, I was no dummy, so for quite a while, I'd been holding back, in one-way or another. You know, deep pocketing some of the money, most of the time I'd leave some pinned to the inside of my shirt then when I got inside I stashed in the fraying fabric of a chair in our room. That evening, I was careless.

"Empty your pockets," Nick demanded. He would not let Solly or me pass him to get inside of the house where it was warm.

"I did," I said.

"You're coming up short," he insisted. I could tell his ire had already formed. Like a bull in a ring preparing to charge, his nostrils flared. "You two worked forty hours between you two. This doesn't add."

I maintained a poker face while I lied, "It's all there."

He looked from me to Solly. "What do you know about this?"

Solly wore a blank look. He said, "I don't know anything."

In disgust, Nick shook his head. "You can say that again."

"Look," I told him. "You got your money."

Nick shot a look over to me that could split rock, but I held myself together. As he advanced toward me, his gaze switched like a light bulb going on. He pushed me down.

"Hey –" Solly began.

"Shut up," Nick said as he raised his hand to him. I hated when he did that. That was worse than the slap itself. I couldn't tell if Solly flinched from my vantage point. I turned over and sought to get back to my feet.

That's when he grabbed me again. He had me by the foot and wrestled my right sneaker off, then my left sneaker. It was there he grabbed the funds.

For a moment, his anger turned to laughter. He kicked his head back as if it were all good fun.

He paid me a back-handed compliment. "You know, Boy, you're pretty smart."

He got like that with me. My name was Jonah; how hard could it be for him to call me that? When he referred to me as 'boy', I knew he wasn't just highlighting my age, it was his way of never letting me forget that I wasn't all the way white.

After Nick quit laughing, he pocketed the money, leaving out one bill, a twenty, which he tore into pieces.

When I stood up, he spat on me to further his spite.

I felt a shiver go up my spine.

What was I going to do?

I swallowed hard.

What could I do?

Nick was a big man, a least a few inches over six feet. Not heavy at all, he was muscular and picked Solly and me up like we were babies. He had both of us by the back of the neck, throttling us; then he crammed our faces way down deep into the snow.

Before I knew what was what, Solly's whole head was so deep into the white it was drowning him. Solly was gasping for air and chunks of the freeze were coughed up each time his father let him up for air.

I was fainting worse because not only was it impossible for me to breathe, but since I had a slimmer neck, Nick could get a tighter grip on me. Kneeling in the chest high snow, Nick bore down with his might. Nick swept up a hand full of snowy gravel and slammed it down into my face. He braced me still and worked the wet and cold rocks into my eyelids, cheeks, and lips—grinding them against my teeth.

I hollered and spat and squirmed, but I could not escape his clutches. Each new fist full of gravel brought a fresh array of scrapping. My flesh tore and seared and stung and all I could do was yelp and buck like a wild horse. I could hear Solly close by his coughing and coughing, it sounded like a lung was coming up.

I wished for a weapon, anything. If only a large rock or fallen branch within grabbing distance, I wouldn't have been so helpless. A few minutes passed, I didn't have the strength to struggle free; I was looking for the stamina to just stay conscious. I did stay alert, barely. After my stepfather let me go, I saw that Solly was in the same bad shape I was.

Like me, he couldn't even make a crawl for it.

Nick strutted in front of the moaning lump of torn meat, which was better known as me and said, "Tell me was that worth it?"

I didn't answer. This already was way past being a bad movie. What was the point?

Then he walked over to Solly and gave him a series of kicks right to his ribs. "And you, Oink, I'm your father. You're barely related to him. Don't you ever side with him over me."

"He didn't know," I managed to get out.

"Shut the fuck up, unless I wanted some more," he told me.

So I shut the fuck up, and there was an end to it.

He walked away, leaving us to our wounds.

In the past after such attacks, I always thought about Solly first, since I was his protector and all, but I admit right then I wasn't thinking about how Solly was doing and then suddenly didn't even care. I was concerned about me. At the very moment when I regained my bearings, I got myself vertical, and I didn't concern myself with helping Solly up.

I just ran.

I ran and ran.

By this time, barely within earshot, I could hear Solly calling after me, asking me where I was going. But, as I ran, I could only hear this faintly and then more faint still till my brother's voice all but disappeared.

In Periot, Wisconsin, the houses were spread out like sailboats along a shoreline. You had to go from one to another. I went heading for the Leland's. I wanted to talk to the man of the house; I needed to borrow something.

Knocking on the door, I nearly collided with Mr. Leland's granddaughter, Lori. Our eyes hooked. She had extraordinary irises of emerald green, intense and searching. She had some books in her mittened hands, and she was all suited up in a coat and scarf as if she was just about to run an errand. She asked me what happened.

"Nothing happened. I'm alright. I'm just here to see your grandpa."

Lori said my face looked like a used razor blade.

"I'm fine," I repeated.

"Sure, you are," she frowned. "Come on, I'll get you something for your cuts," she said, taking my arm.

I pushed her away. "No, I want to see your grandpa."

She knitted her brows together and told me Mr. Leland was around the back in the shed.

I walked around to the back, slowly, with measured steps. It was hitting me now. I felt so queasy in the core of my stomach. My fear bubbled. I kept waiting for a pop. *How in the Hell was I going to ask for this?*

I approached Mr. Leland's bent figure. Over a sanding board, he was just filing away. He didn't notice me till I was right up on him. He was a funny looking old man. Stocky as a bulldog, he wore his graying blond hair in a ponytail. He straightened up when he saw me and put his hand to his lower back. He shook his head in a pitying manner.

"Why don't you just stay out of his way?" he asked me.

"It's not so easy, Mr. Leland."

He tilted his head to the side and told me, "You don't have to make it this hard."

"You think I asked for this?"

"All I'm saying is you gotta do what he says. Everything he says. Maybe you've heard that old saying: the life you save may be your own."

"I've heard it," I said.

Pause. Then more silence as he peered into me more deeply.

"Where's your other half? Where's Solly?"

"I left him," I said, taking a visual sweep of the room. "It's all right though. The storm is over."

He nodded and frowned. "Why don't you go inside? My wife will clean you up. She's in there making a pie. You can stay --"

"I didn't come all the way over here for pie, Mr. Leland. Or to get cleaned up."

He nodded again, this time more slowly. "Well, then, what did you come here for?"

"I came here for a loan."

"Sure, sure. Take what you want. You know, I promised you many years ago I'd always been here for you and your brother. What do you want?"

I didn't hesitate for an instant.

"That," I said and pointed to his gun rack.

He turned and looked behind him. "That?"

"Yep."

"Well, this is a fine time to think about that? You want to hunt, now? When I took you boys out last month --"

"I ain't hunting."

"Say what? Are you crazy? You want a rifle, but you don't want to hunt with it? What are you talking about? That man must have hit you too hard in the head."

I smirked. It was funny because if anything the sense had finally gotten knocked into me, not the other way around. At last after many episodes, I was going to move from a defensive posture to an offensive one.

This is why I picked Mr. Leland. He was an old soldier, Vietnam and all that, so he knew all about shooting and shot positions. Since Lori had little interest and he didn't have a grandson, he had shown Solly and me everything about how to wield a rifle, even how to fire from a prone position. I guess it was only natural of me to turn to him at a time like this.

"I'm thinking clearly, Mr. Leland, I need a gun for protection. I'm not going to get beat like this ever again."

More silence followed. I shattered it by telling him that I'd been thinking of this for a good long time.

Mr. Leland's color rose but his smallish, green eyes didn't tell me anything. He shook his head. "You don't want what you're asking for. You're fixing on doing something you're going to be sorry for."

I nodded. "I'm just going to have to be sorry then."

"Wait a minute. Have you thought this through? I mean really thought this through. This ain't the way. This ain't you, Jonah. You don't go around doing rash things."

"Mr. Leland, I have thought this through --"

He talked over me, speaking quickly using wild hand gestures. "Jonah, I've been mad. I've been crazy mad, but you have to believe me that sometimes the smartest thing to do is to hold your fire."

"Mr. Leland, I don't have any fire. That's what I'm here about."

"Look, you and Solly, I know you have had it rough, but this ain't no way. You're about to blow this thing sky high…

You two made it this far; just keep doing what you're doing. Don't do this, I'm begging you."

I shook my head. "Don't beg, Mr. Leland."

"I will beg you. I will. I am begging you."

"You're begging me and my brother to wait –"

"Yes, wait."

"With all due respect," I said as I eyed the rack of weapons, again. "But it's gotten past waiting. Who knows what's going to happen next? I don't want to get hurt or worse and I don't want to see my brother hurt or worse and that's it. End of story."

"But it's not the end. You do this, and it's only the beginning."

"My mind is made up. It's set. If you don't want to help me, don't. I'll get it from someplace else. This is Peroit; everyone has a gun, except for the people who need one."

I was prepared to leave right then when he again said, "Don't do it."

My brown eyes met his green ones, which were just like Lori's emerald, searching. I wished he'd cut it with all the grave concern. All it did was add another layer to things that were already deep enough.

"All right, I won't take it," I said to him but that was a lie. A big one. As soon as Mr. Leland turned his back to go inside, I knew I had only a short period of time to get what I'd come for.

In every bad situation, there's always time to act but only a second or two before the cliché comes true, bad goes to worse.

I walked toward a side cupboard. The floorboards creaked beneath my footsteps. I opened a drawer and pulled out a short heavy revolver. They call this type of weapon with its snub nose. It's also called a belly gun because it's just right to shove against someone's stomach. And sure there was nothing brave or noble about anything I was doing – stealing, plotting a murder, etc. But I wasn't aiming for those descriptions. What's the use of honor? I'd rather be safe.

Maybe this would work out for the best because a small weapon is more portable and I figured Mr. Leland won't notice it missing for a while since as far as he knew my interest was in his rifle.

I took the gun and slipped out with it.

It felt good to be out in the air.

Out of the corner of my eye, I saw the large white clouds floating across the sky. I caught my breath. Though I had secured what I'd come for, I knew this was just the start of things. Mr. Leland sure got that part right.

I came in like a cat burglar. I clawed at the pane until I was able to squeeze through. Solly walked by, just as I fell to the floor. In surprise, he nearly dropped the large can of ravioli he was finishing.

Solly and I had the exact opposite way of diffusing stress. He ate, and I didn't. At least so far, he hadn't turned into a blimp, and I hadn't gone full manorexic.

"What's wrong with the front door?" he asked.

"I saw his pick-up. I thought he'd come back."

"Naw, he ain't here," Solly told me in between shoveling down spoonfuls. You'd think he'd grown up in a great big family where you have to stake your claim early. His habit of eating fast was so that barely even pausing to breathe was his way of keeping the food warm. "Where did you go?" he asked.

"I went over to Mr. Leland's."

"Did you see Lori?"

"Yeah."

Solly smirked.

"What are you smirking about?"

"Nothing… She likes you."

I didn't answer his lead. I went into the bathroom and got my first look at the damage. My lip busted pink and purple. My whole pan was bloody with lacerations.

"Did you hear what I said?" Solly called after me.

"Yes, I did." I wet a small towel, so I could use it as a warm compress.

From the other room, I could hear Solly still on the same topic. "Lori's not bad looking. She talks too much, but she has pretty eyes."

"I don't have time for girls; I've got too many problems," I told him flatly, but in a muffled voice on the count of I was holding the cloth to my mouth. "Besides she'd be better paired with you," I said, thinking of her wide mouth and dizzily curling blond hair.

"Don't push her off on me. I got just as many problems as you have."

And we were silent again.

I came back to the room and sat on the bed. I felt a little more composed. I was at least breathing steady. "Let me see your ribs," I said to him. That was the last thing I recalled from the attack, his father kicking him there.

Solly came closer to me and lifted his tee shirt. What I saw was definite, half-moon shaped bruises made from his father's boots—tip and the heel.

"How does it feel? Sore?"

Solly nodded. "How does it look? Do you see any swelling?"

Solly was a husky kid, so the words: "No more than usual," slipped out of my mouth though I didn't mean it the flip way it sounded. If his ribs felt anything like my face, it didn't matter how meaty he was built, he must be in real pain. I laid my hand against the skin there to see if I could feel any heat. Pain draws heat, and there was radiating heat coming off his skin. I began to worry.

"Maybe we should swing by the hospital?'

"That's too much waiting. We'd be there half the night."

"But, I can't tell. I ain't a doctor. Maybe there is really something wrong. Remember before --"

"Of course, I remember before. How could I forget when I had to wear that thing for two months?"

"Solly, maybe you have some broken ribs or something."

"They can't put a cast on my ribs, can they?"

"No."

"Then how do they fix it?"

"I think they tape it."

Solly put his hand up as if to say he didn't want to hear it. "Skip it. I don't want to be taped."

He pulled his shirt down and ate the last of the ravioli.

"Solly..." I began to whine. I hated to whine, but I was so tired and achy and cold and pissed off. I just wanted some cooperation from him. I only wanted to help. I laid back on the bed totally forgetting that it was there I had hidden the gun. It was between my waistband and the back of my jeans.

I quickly sat bolt upright. I removed the weapon I had secured to my lower back.

Still not noticing, Solly chucked the empty can in the trash. Its clank made a violent sound.

I held up the weapon for him to plainly see it. "I got this."

"That's a gun," he said after a double take.

I nodded.

"Is it loaded?"

"Not yet."

He motioned to me to let him hold it.

I did without reminding him to treat it like it was armed even though it wasn't because I knew he already knew that.

Solly held it for a while, examining it. He checked the chamber and said to me, "It's cute."

"Cute?" I asked. Of all the adjectives in the world, how did that one pop into his mind to describe a weapon?

I gave it a deeper look.

"Yeah, who'd think that something so small could actually hurt someone. But it'll get the job done."

I said taking it from his hands.

"What job?"

I got up, placing the gun on the desk. I began to pace.

"I didn't even know Mr. Leland had this type," Solly said. "I thought he just had hunting stuff."

"He's pretty well armed."

"Why?" Solly laughed and winced. He ain't in Alpha company anymore."

"I suppose, he's got to protect his wife and Lori."

Solly frowned, now holding his side. "He must have like twenty or thirty guns. That's real stupid."

"What's stupid about it?"

"He only has two hands."

I stopped pacing. "I guess it helps him to sleep nights."

"Is that what you got the gun for, Jonah," Solly asked, "Sleeping?"

That made me think. I mean really think and think and think and think. I thought until I was trembling all over and my head felt dizzy.

"Jonah? Jonah? Earth to Jonah? Come in Jonah?" Solly kept asking. He clapped his hands in front of me.

I snapped back into the present.

For a second or two, I took stock of his face noticing how clear and boyish it looked for a change. It wasn't acne that so often polluted his complexion since his father had been back. Usually after a beating, Solly was so bruised up that his face was distorted and outsized. This time he looked like himself, with his delicate features. How his father called him an Oink was beyond me. His nose especially was finely cut to even be mistaken for a snout. It looked like something a plastic surgeon would construct, a showpiece even.

"What's the job?" he asked me.

"Huh?" was my reply.

"You planning to stick-up a bank?"

I gave a nervous laugh then took a deep breath then spoke in a blue streak. "I've had it with your father, Solly. Ever since he came back he's been flying into his rages on us. I'm sick of being boot kicked and bitch slapped and thrown across the room. This shit has been going on for too long. Today, just capped it off," I told him. "Why can't we keep our own money? We earned it. That man wants everything. Everything. And I'm sick of it."

Solly's mouth was open. Then, he closed it. Then he gestured to the gun, "So what does the gun have to do with that?"

"I just told you, Solly, we're getting out."

"Out? Where out?" he asked.

"He'll cripple us if we don't."

"We can't leave. We can't leave Ma. What about her?"

I went back to pacing. I thought long before I spoke then considering heavily if I really wanted to say this next part. "What about her?" I asked finally.

Solly looked at me incredulously. "Well, we just can't leave her behind."

"She's the reason we're in this mess."

"How do you figure that?"

"She hasn't done one goddamn thing --"

"She's doing the best she can -–"

"This is the best that she can do," I said lifting up his shirt.

He jerked my hands away. "That's not her fault."

"Yeah, right. She doesn't have to keep taking him back. She could stop this if she wanted to."

"What do you want her to do?" Solly asked.

"You're not listening to me," I shouted at him.

"I am listening," he shouted back.

"Then why are you talking?!"

Solly gave me a piercing look and went quiet.

I began, "Last week, I promise myself the next time he puts his hands on us, he's dead --"

"Don't you have that kind of bass backwards? The next time –"

I spoke over him. "-- What did I say about talking?"

He went quiet again.

"I got a gun, and I plan to use it."

This time he waited a good few seconds before he asked, "On my father?"

"Yes, Solly, yes," I said. "On your father."

At that instant, Solly's skin turned sweaty and clammy. "You decided this all last week, and you didn't clue me in before now?"

I nodded. "I know it is a lot to get down all at once."

"You only had a week to think of it… Jonah, you're really going to kill him? Like shoot him in the head or something?"

I shrugged (those were some blunt questions he was asking me). "I'll do what I need to do."

Solly didn't have much of a reaction after that. He just glanced away for a moment. He looked toward the window.

Outside, the dull yellow sun had set and pitch had settled in for the night.

Solly's eyes came back to mine. He said, "Good."

About the Author

A Whittenberg is a Philadelphia native who has a global perspective. If she wasn't an author she'd be a private detective or a jazz singer. She loves reading about history and true crime and travels broadly. Her novels include *Sweet Thang, Hollywood and Maine, Life is Fine*, and *Tutored*.

Apprentice
House Press
Loyola University Maryland

Apprentice House is the country's only campus-based, student-staffed book publishing company. Directed by professors and industry professionals, it is a nonprofit activity of the Communication Department at Loyola University Maryland.

Using state-of-the-art technology and an experiential learning model of education, Apprentice House publishes books in untraditional ways. This dual responsibility as publishers and educators creates an unprecedented collaborative environment among faculty and students, while teaching tomorrow's editors, designers, and marketers.

Outside of class, progress on book projects is carried forth by the AH Book Publishing Club, a co-curricular campus organization supported by Loyola University Maryland's Office of Student Activities.

Eclectic and provocative, Apprentice House titles intend to entertain as well as spark dialogue on a variety of topics. Financial contributions to sustain the press's work are welcomed. Contributions are tax deductible to the fullest extent allowed by the IRS.

To learn more about Apprentice House books or to obtain submission guidelines, please visit www.apprenticehouse.com.

Apprentice House
Communication Department
Loyola University Maryland
4501 N. Charles Street
Baltimore, MD 21210
Ph: 410-617-5265
info@apprenticehouse.com
www.apprenticehouse.com

www.ingramcontent.com/pod-product-compliance
Lightning Source LLC
Chambersburg PA
CBHW071436260626
47170CB00008B/2737